HELLO . . . AND GOODBYE

Fargo pulled the trigger and watched the bullet plunk through the man's lower chest. The bullet exited his back and spanged off a rock, painting it bloodred.

He screamed and clutched his back, triggering his pistol into the ground. The report hadn't even faded when the Trailsman rammed another shell into the Henry's breech and swung back to the other shooter.

The man glared up at the Trailsman, jaw slack, sweat runneling the grime on his gray-bristled face. "Wh-who the hell are you an'—an' why the hell can't you mind your own *business*?"

"Name's Fargo." The Trailsman punched a slug through the man's right temple, slamming him back into the dirt.

THE
TRAILSMAN
#298

DEAD MAN'S
BOUNTY

by

Jon Sharpe

Ⓢ
A SIGNET BOOK

SIGNET
Published by New American Library, a division of
Penguin Group (USA) Inc., 375 Hudson Street,
New York, New York 10014, USA
Penguin Group (Canada), 90 Eglinton Avenue East, Suite 700, Toronto,
Ontario M4P 2Y3, Canada (a division of Pearson Penguin Canada Inc.)
Penguin Books Ltd., 80 Strand, London WC2R 0RL, England
Penguin Ireland, 25 St. Stephen's Green, Dublin 2,
Ireland (a division of Penguin Books Ltd.)
Penguin Group (Australia), 250 Camberwell Road, Camberwell, Victoria 3124,
Australia (a division of Pearson Australia Group Pty. Ltd.)
Penguin Books India Pvt. Ltd., 11 Community Centre, Panchsheel Park,
New Delhi - 110 017, India
Penguin Group (NZ), cnr Airborne and Rosedale Roads, Albany,
Auckland 1310, New Zealand (a division of Pearson New Zealand Ltd.)
Penguin Books (South Africa) (Pty.) Ltd., 24 Sturdee Avenue,
Rosebank, Johannesburg 2196, South Africa

Penguin Books Ltd., Registered Offices:
80 Strand, London WC2R 0RL, England

First published by Signet, an imprint of New American Library,
a division of Penguin Group (USA) Inc.

First Printing, August 2006
10   9   8   7   6   5   4   3   2   1

The first chapter of this book previously appeared in *South Texas Slaughter,*
the two hundred ninety-seventh volume in this series.

 REGISTERED TRADEMARK—MARCA REGISTRADA

Printed in the United States of America

PUBLISHER'S NOTE
This is a work of fiction. Names, characters, places, and incidents either are
the product of the author's imagination or are used fictitiously, and any resem-
blance to actual persons, living or dead, events, or locales is entirely
coincidental.

   The publisher does not have any control over and does not assume any
responsibility for author or third-party Web sites or their content.

The Trailsman

Beginnings . . . they bend the tree and they mark the man. Skye Fargo was born when he was eighteen. Terror was his midwife, vengeance his first cry. Killing spawned Skye Fargo, ruthless, cold-blooded murder. Out of the acrid smoke of gunpowder still hanging in the air, he rose, cried out a promise never forgotten.

The Trailsman they began to call him all across the West: searcher, scout, hunter, the man who could see where others only looked, his skills for hire but not his soul, the man who lived each day to the fullest, yet trailed each tomorrow. Skye Fargo, the Trailsman, the seeker who could take the wildness of a land and the wanting of a woman and make them his own.

Colorado, 1860—
one corpse, two fillies from Heart's Desire,
and a whole heap of trouble.

1

The tall, dark rider reined his horse to a sudden halt. Hand flicking to the Colt .44 on his right hip, he squinted his lake blue eyes at the rocky butte rising in the south—sun-blasted and stippled with sage and dwarf piñons.

Fargo had heard something.

The Ovaro pinto beneath him had heard it, too. The horse held its head high, ears pricked, eyes wary.

Another faint crack, like a twig snapping, sounded on the other side of the scarp. Muffled by distance, it was still louder than the previous gunshot. Whoever the shooter was, he was heading toward Fargo.

The Trailsman, as he was known throughout the frontier, swung his right leg over the saddle horn, kicked his left boot from its stirrup, and slid straight down to the ground. Dropping the pinto's reins, he quickly shucked his Henry repeater from its saddle boot and grabbed a spyglass from his saddlebags. Hanging the glass around his neck by a leather thong, he jacked a .44 round into the Henry's chamber, then jogged around behind the horse and began climbing the scarp.

The big, broad-shouldered man, clad in buckskins,

undershot boots, and a broad-brimmed hat, a red bandanna knotted around his neck, moved with a mountain lion's quiet grace.

Gaining the crest's bank in no time, he doffed his hat and lay between two boulders. Keeping his head low, he stared southward through the spyglass, using a spindly sage clump to shield the lens from the sun.

A mile south, a little-used freight trail ran along a tree-lined wash. Along the trail, what looked like a small buckboard wagon was barreling along behind a stocky horse or a mule. From this distance, even through the spyglass, the animal and wagon were little more than a brown blur behind which a sand-colored dust cloud rose.

Smoke puffed over the wagon. A half second later, a rifle crack reached the Trailsman's ears.

Tightening the spyglass's focus, Fargo saw that one of the two people in the wagon was firing a rifle at something behind them. Sliding the glass westward, Fargo saw a half dozen horseback riders crest a low hill and gallop down the other side, making a beeline for the wagon.

The riders whooped and hollered, firing pistols and rifles at the fleeing buckboard.

Fargo cursed and shortened the spyglass to include a broader field of vision. The trail would take the wagon around the east side of the scarp. If Fargo hurried, he might be able to cut off the pursuers and find out what the hoorahing was all about—if it was about anything and not just a passel of bored hardcases hornswoggling a couple of hapless farmers.

Fargo was down the scarp in half the time it had taken him to climb it.

He slipped the Henry back in its boot, the glass back in the saddlebags, and swung into the saddle. Putting his spurs to the pinto, he galloped straight along his previous course, the scarp falling away to his right, the trail appearing ahead. He swung the Ovaro onto the trail and stopped, peering south as his own dust caught up to him.

He could see little but the trail disappearing over the brow of a low rise.

A scream rose. A mule brayed.

Pistols cracked over men's jubilant whoops.

The thunderclap of a wagon tipping pricked the hair along the back of the Trailsman's neck.

Skye Fargo spurred the Ovaro into a gallop. Horse and rider bolted over the low rise. Spying the overturned wagon in a sage-carpeted flat ahead and left of the wagon trail, Fargo reined the Ovaro toward the wreck, giving the horse its head.

The wagon lay on its side, near a line of pines curving along the base of low buttes and a creek. Contents from the wagon box lay strewn for twenty yards across the flat. The wagon's two raised wheels were still spinning. The mule lay on its side, tangled in its traces, blood glistening at the back of its head.

Fargo poked his index finger through the Henry's trigger guard when female screams rose amidst the men's laughter. He saw one of the attackers drop his trousers and raise the skirts of one of the fallen women, a blonde, while three men chased the other woman toward the creek.

The second woman, a brunette, was topless. One of her pursuers whipped a cream-colored blouse over his head as he chased her.

"No! Damn you!" the woman near the wagon protested before a sharp backhanded slap knocked her flat against the side of the buckboard. "Get your filthy hands off me!"

Hearing the Ovaro's thundering hooves, two men rummaging through the spilled contents of the wagon spun toward Fargo, alarm flashing across their bearded, sun-seared faces. As they reached for the pistols jutting from their hips, Fargo snapped the Henry to his shoulder.

The Trailsman had fired from the pinto's hurricane deck enough times that he timed the shots precisely to the stallion's fluid gate.

Both men danced backward, screaming, dropping their pistols, and hitting the ground in unison.

Smoking Henry in hand, Fargo leaped from the saddle while the Ovaro continued running on past the dead mule and the wagon. The Trailsman stopped, dropped to a knee, and aimed the rifle toward the man with the blonde.

The man turned toward Fargo, his pants down around his ankles, his member jutting up between his drooping shirttails. Hatless, he held a pistol down near his right thigh, staring toward Fargo with an angry, befuddled expression on his mustachioed face.

"What in Christ?" the man barked. "Who the hell're you?"

"Drop the shootin' iron," Fargo called from one knee, his rifle butt snugged to his cheek.

"Like hell!"

The man raised the pistol and stepped forward. Before he could level the .36, he tripped over his pants and his longhandles and stumbled forward, triggering the .36 into the ground halfway between him and Fargo. The Trailsman triggered his own shot as the man fell, the bullet cutting the air over and right of the hardcase's head.

Lying on his right hip, raging, the man raised the revolver. As he thumbed the hammer back, Fargo's Henry spoke. The slug plunked through the center of the hardcase's forehead, an inch above his bushy black brows, exiting his skull with a spray of brains, bone, and blood. The man fell back, staring sightlessly at the sky as his legs kicked spasmodically.

Fargo glanced at the blonde.

She sat with her feet bare and legs spread, skirt still bunched around her waist. She wasn't wearing pantaloons, only a skimpy pair of lacy pink underpants

4

that the hardcase had torn in half, revealing the creamy curve of her left hip rising to a narrow waist.

In too much shock to bother covering her long, shapely legs, she glanced from Fargo to the dead hardcase, then back again, her sandy brows bunched with befuddlement. Weed flecks clung to her long curly hair. Blood trickled from a crack in her upper lip.

A pistol spoke. A slug kicked up dirt a yard from Fargo's left boot.

"Oh!" the blonde cried.

Fargo turned toward the shot. The two men who'd been chasing the brunette were now running toward the Trailsman, their pistols held high, long dusters flapping around their legs. The hat of the man on the right blew off as, running, he leveled the revolver, squinted down the barrel, and fired.

The slug sizzled past Fargo's left ear.

As the other man fired, Fargo levered a fresh shell into his Henry's breech. He snapped off an errant shot and then, intending to remove the blonde from the line of fire, traced a serpentine course toward the overturned wagon, keeping the old buckboard between him and the two approaching hardcases.

As he ducked down behind the wagon's undercarriage, a bullet clanked and sparked off the iron-rimmed rear wheel. Another drilled through the box, missing Fargo by a hairbreadth. Tightening his jaws, he snaked the Henry over the wagon, aimed at the man approaching on his left, and drilled a ragged hole through the man's left shoulder.

The man screamed a curse and dropped to his knees, grabbing his bloody shoulder with the hand holding the six-shooter. Fargo ejected the spent shell, loaded another, and swung the rifle toward the other hardcase.

As the man shouted, *"Son of a bitch!"* and triggered a round through the slack of the Trailsman's left shirtsleeve, Fargo pulled the trigger and watched the bullet

5

plunk through the man's lower chest. The bullet exited his lower back and spanged off a rock, painting it bloodred.

He screamed and clutched his back, triggering his pistol into the ground. The report hadn't yet faded when the Trailsman rammed another shell into the Henry's breech and swung back to the other shooter.

The man glared up at the Trailsman, jaw slack, sweat runneling the grime on his gray-bristled face. "Wh-who the hell are you an'—an' why the hell can't you mind your own *business*?"

"Name's Fargo." The Trailsman punched a slug through the man's right temple, slamming him back into the dirt.

Fargo turned to the other man and aimed the Henry. The man stared back at him, face bunched with pain and exasperation, small eyes open wide. Fargo raked, "Didn't your momma ever teach you how to act around girls?"

"No, wait!" the man cried.

Fargo sent a slug careening through his left cheekbone and watched the man's quivering head follow half his brainpan onto the gravel and sage behind him.

He looked around.

All the hardcases were down and unmoving, their horses and Fargo's pinto grazing back in the pines lining the creek. Fargo lowered his Henry and tramped over to where the blonde lay in the sage where he'd last seen her. She looked around dumbly, let her gaze stray up to the tall, dark stranger. Fargo returned the appraisal, his heart giving a little hitch at all that thick blond hair curling down her shoulders, at the cobalt blue eyes and small, round breasts pushing at the dusty orange blouse ripped halfway down her lightly freckled chest.

When his eyes trailed down from her wasp waist to her bare, creamy legs and small, fine-boned feet looking so pink and delicate amidst the gravel and sage, she gave a haughty chuff and jerked her skirt down over her knees and feet. Her eyes snapped wide, the veil of befuddlement lifting, and she turned to where the other girl lay at the edge of the pines.

"Charity!"

The blonde pushed herself up and, holding her skirt above her bare feet with one hand, wove around shrubs and large rocks as she ran toward the creek. Fargo glanced at the torn pink underpants she'd left on a tuft of silverthorn. His cheek twitched wryly, and he turned to follow her.

The girl's feet must be hard-soled as Modoc moccasins. She didn't falter once in spite of the tough, brown, prickly weeds and gravel.

She knelt beside the other girl called Charity, took the girl's hand in her own, and called her name. Fargo stopped behind the blonde. The brunette lay on her back. Her thick brown hair had partially fallen from the prim bun atop her head and hung in dusty ringlets about her finely sculpted, full-lipped face. The girl's blouse and corset lay in the weeds a good distance away. Her deep, full, round breasts, pale as new-fallen snow and tipped with red-brown nipples, cast oval shadows down her belly.

The blonde sobbed and, clutching Charity's hand in both of hers, lowered her head over the unconscious girl's chest. "Charity! Oh, God, Charity—*please don't die!*"

She must have seen Fargo's shadow angling across Charity's legs. She whipped her head around and looked up at him, her blue eyes tear filled, brows furled with exasperation. "Would you please quit staring at her breasts and *do* something!"

2

Fargo set his rifle down and nudged the blonde aside. Kneeling over Charity, he thumbed each eyelid back in turn, peering into her liquid brown eyes, then lowered an ear to her chest, listening.

"Is she alive?" the blonde intoned. "Oh, God, tell me she's alive. She's all I have in the world!"

Fargo slid his left hand under Charity's head, lifted it slightly, saw the flat rock beneath, felt the goose egg rising beneath the girl's scalp. He gentled her head back to the rock, then slipped his left arm under her neck. He snaked his right arm under the girl's legs, and stood with her draped across his forearms.

"What are you doing?" the blonde beseeched, leaping back and turning to follow Fargo with her eyes. "Oh, good heavens—is she dead? Please tell me she's not dead!"

"Don't get your panties twisted," Fargo said as he carried Charity into the cool, dark shade of the pines. He chuffed, remembering the skimpy pink drawers the blonde had left in the brush. "Uh, sorry. I mean, skirt."

She trotted behind him, breathing sharply, pausing

to scoop the brunette's chemise off a sage bush. "Where are you going? What are you doing?"

"Charity just needs a little cold water's all," Fargo said, moving through the trees and stepping across the rocks to the sun-dappled creek.

The fresh smell of the pines and the high-country snowmelt filled his nostrils, washing out the stench of cordite and death. He knelt in a sandy place among the rocks, at the edge of the water, and lowered the girl gently to the flood-scalloped sand. He slipped the bandanna from around his neck, plunged it into the creek, then wrung it out on Charity's forehead.

As soon as the cold water hit her, the brunette's head moved and her full lips shaped a wince. Her eyes fluttered.

"She's alive!" the blonde quietly exclaimed, kneeling to Fargo's left and nervously wringing her hands together as she stared down at Charity.

Fargo resoaked the bandanna, then wrung it out again on Charity's forehead. The freshwater dribbled into her eyes and down her classically sculpted cheeks, dampening the sand beneath her head. Charity groaned and moved her head from side to side. Her eyes opened, stared blindly at the sky for a moment.

Her gaze fixed on Fargo's broad, beard-stubbled face. Her eyelids snapped wide, her pupils expanding with horror.

"No! Leave me—"

"It's okay, Charity," the blonde said, taking the brunette in her arms and hugging her. "He's a friend."

"No, it's *them*!"

The blonde rocked Charity in her arms, cooing gently. "Shhhh. He won't hurt you. I don't know his name, but he really saved our bacon."

"Oh, Lord," Charity said, the fear in her eyes abating. She glanced around, bewildered, wincing from the pain no doubt lancing her skull. "Where . . . What happened? I vaguely remember shooting, and then the wagon . . ." Her eyes flashed shock and horror as she whipped her head around, hair flying. "Where's Father?"

"Oh, God—I don't know," the blonde said, a nervous trill in her voice as she pulled away from Charity. "I'm sure he's all right. Can I leave you here while I look for him?"

Charity glanced at Fargo standing over them. He shuttled curious glances between them. Father?

He returned his glance to Charity as she dipped her chin toward her exposed breasts. Mouth and eyes gaping, she gave a horrified scream and crossed her arms over her chest, snapping her head up at Fargo accusingly.

"Here," the blonde said, tossing the chemise to Charity, who grabbed it and clutched it to her tightly, her eyes blazing defensively up at the brawny stranger towering over her. She hadn't covered herself completely, and a half-moon portion of her left breast bulged out from beneath the sheer silk garment.

"I'll go check on Father," said the blonde as she wheeled and ran back through the pines, heading for the wagon.

Fargo stared after her, his brows beetled. He hadn't seen anyone else in the wagon. He turned to the brunette staring up at him while pressing the chemise so tight to her body that both breasts were now bulging out from beneath.

"A little late for modesty," he grunted. "I done seen 'em, and believe me, girl, you got nothin' to be ashamed of." He gave her a wink and started after the blonde. "You sit tight."

The blonde was halfway back to the wagon, striding swiftly on her bare feet, before Fargo reached her. "When I spied you, there weren't but two people in the wagon. Your old man must've fallen out a good ways back along—"

"Oh, no," said the blonde, pointing and quickening her stride. "There he is!"

She jogged ahead, stepping amongst the trunks and crates, carpetbags, and foodstuffs fallen from the overturned wagon. One of the steamer trunks had burst open, and ladies' dresses and high-button shoes and silk underwear and stockings were strewn as if fallen from the sky.

That must be why Fargo hadn't seen the coffin before now.

The hand-hewn pine box lay on its side, looking bizarrely incongruous amidst the delicate clothes and perfume bottles, one of which had broken, filling the air with a pungent dose of rose petals. The blonde knelt on the other side of the coffin, shoving aside the lid and a powder blue wrapper to reveal a skinny hombre lying belly-down on the ground, legs straight, arms clinging tautly to his sides. His curly red hair, parted in the middle and carefully combed, hung over his ears to his shoulders.

"Papa," the blonde said, snaking her arms beneath him and lifting with a slight grunt. "I'm so sorry, Papa."

The man rolled stiffly onto his back. He could have been a board, for all the movement he made, his arms and legs remaining snugged to his body. His eyes were lightly closed, the red lashes and brushy red mustache looking especially dark against his gaunt, chalky face.

He was impeccably dressed in a crisp pin-striped shirt, rose-colored cravat, brocade vest, and a black frock coat that sagged slightly on his narrow, bony shoulders. His slacks were pin-striped broadcloth of the highest quality. His high-heeled boots were black, hand-tooled and polished to a high shine.

From two tied-down black holsters jutted the pearl grips of a matched pair of silver-plated .44 Navies.

Fargo's admiring gaze remained glued to the shooting irons, far prettier by half than three-quarters of the women he'd bedded. He couldn't help giving a soft whistle. "Last time I saw a pair of pistols like that, it was on the hips of Three-Gun Pete LeFleur."

The blonde had picked up the man's pearl gray hat and was reshaping it with her hands. "Help me get him back into his box, will you?"

Fargo chuffed. What he didn't get himself into. He knelt at the head of the corpse and gripped it under the shoulders while the blonde took the feet. Fargo counted to three, and they swung the cadaver up and over the side of the coffin, laying it gently inside.

While the woman lifted his head to place his hat down snug on the combed red curls, Fargo's handsome, sun-seasoned features acquired an incredulous look. "Holy shit. That *is* Three-Gun Pete LeFleur." He looked at the girl. "He's your old man?"

The blonde was adjusting the hat on the corpse's head. Fargo could see from her profile that her cheeks were brushed with red, but she was trying to maintain a casual expression while she tipped the hat first this way, then that. "Why doesn't it look right now? Doggone it, anyway!"

"I haven't heard of ol' Three-Gun in years. Figured he'd been turned toe-down a long time ago."

"Well, he wasn't!" the blonde said, turning to him angrily. "He's been living a good, clean life as Charles LaForge, proprietor and manager of the Hog's Head Saloon in Heart's Desire. Leastways, he was till a damn bounty hunter recognized him three days ago." Her voice broke, and she tightened her jaws as she looked at the old, dead gunfighter sadly and flicked dust from his vest.

"Bounty hunter took him down, eh?"

"Yes, but he didn't collect the bounty!" She whipped her face toward Fargo again, blond curls flying, face pinched with fury. "Now the scoundrel is as dead as poor Papa. I shot him myself, just after he shot Papa. Blew his head clean off and tossed him down an old privy hole!"

The Trailsman eyed her with fascination and scratched his head. "You don't say."

"Just said so, didn't I?"

"And who are these fine gentlemen?" Fargo asked, running his gaze across the six dead men strewn about the flat. "More bounty hunters, I take it?"

The blonde straightened and turned, fists on her hips, to regard the bloody corpse of the man who'd tried to savage her. "I reckon," she said with disgust. "The man who shot Papa whooped and hollered how he'd taken down Three-Gun Pete before I had time to pull Papa's third gun out from under the bar and drill the bastard good. Word spread from there, I reckon."

"Where you takin' him?"

"Del Norte." The blonde strode toward the dead bounty hunter. "It was Papa's wish to be buried there with his brother, Karl."

"Ah, Karl," Fargo drawled, nodding. "Killed by a sheriff's posse, if my memory serves. After him and your old man robbed the bank in Taos."

The blonde, standing over the bounty hunter, brought her bare right foot back, then forward, planting her curled toes solidly against the man's left cheek. "Damn you!" His head jerked to the side and slowly turned back.

"How much your old man have on his head?"

Fists balled at her sides, the blonde stared down at the dead bounty man. Slowly, her shoulders relaxed. "The old wanted dodger I seen said ten thousand dollars."

"Dead or alive, I take it."

She nodded. "Issued by some express company back east."

"That's what happens when you prey on every stage

line in Illinois, Missouri, and Arkansas for ten years straight, and kill half a dozen express guards."

She wheeled on him again. "Papa never killed anyone that didn't try to shoot him first. It was Karl who started the killin'. Then Papa had to hone his draw to protect himself, with so many lynch mobs and uncouth lawmen fogging his trail. Besides, he's been peaceful as a kitten for the past six years."

Fargo ran his gaze up and down the girl's lithe frame, and slitted his eyes as he shook his head and smiled crookedly. "I sure never woulda guessed ol' Three-Gun Pete had a couple daughters that looked like you two."

She flushed and pulled her torn dress closed across the small, round breasts, the fabric creasing around the nipples. Her eyes were wary. "You are a gentleman, aren't you?"

"Name's Fargo. You can call me Skye. And no, I ain't a gentleman. But, unlike these boys"—the Trailsman glanced at the dead men, then let his eyes stray back to the girl's heaving chest—"I don't take candy that ain't offered."

Fargo noticed the girl staring back at him, a wistful cast to her cobalt blues as they lingered on the buckskin tunic stretched taut across the twin slabs of his chest, at the brown hair poking through the rawhide ties. They fell lower, to the hard flatness of his belly, and lower still, before her cheeks colored like those of a girl who'd just seen something in the boys' privy that both confused her and threatened the vapors.

Chagrined, she brushed a lock of blond hair back from her face and turned to the dead mule.

"I don't know how we're going to get Papa to Del Norte without a mule," she said, heaving a sigh.

Fargo looked around at the mule, the overturned wagon, the coffin, and enough strewn dresses to clothe half the society ladies in Saint Louis. He matched the blonde's sigh and stooped to retrieve the coffin's lid.

Fitting the lid over the box, pounding the edges with the heel of his hand, he said, "You'd best stay here tonight. Your sis ain't gonna be up for traveling, and it'll be dark soon, anyway. While you tidy up, I'll try to right your wagon and park her down by the water."

The blonde sounded a little breathless as she looked up at him from a crouch. "You . . . you're going to help us?"

"Don't see anyone else around but dead men." He gave the lid another punch with the heel of his hand. "I'll get you to the little crossroads town up yonder, and you can figure it out from there."

"Thank you, Mr. Fargo."

He placed two fingers in his mouth and whistled. A hundred yards off in the trees, the Ovaro lifted its head with a start and turned toward Fargo. The Trailsman whistled again, and the horse came trotting, its reins trailing.

"Call me Skye."

"You can call me Harmony, on account of how that's my name." She chuckled.

Fargo looked at her. She walked around the wagon wreckage, gathering clothes and perfume bottles, her wheat yellow hair hanging over her face, her blouse hanging open to expose even more cleavage than he'd seen before.

"Figures ol' Three-Gun'd have a girl named Harmony who's good with a six-shooter," Fargo muttered. "What don't figure is he'd have one that looked like *you*."

3

With his lariat dallied around the pinto's saddle horn, and plenty of pushing and shoving and levering with stout cottonwood branches, Fargo righted the girls' wagon. When he'd helped Harmony reload the coffin, steamer trunks, carpetbags, and gunnysacks, he harnessed the pinto to the wagon, and led the horse and rattling schooner to the pine shade along the creek.

Charity was resting, still looking dazed, against a boulder, soaking her feet in the water. She'd donned a fresh white blouse. The brunette's feet were as pretty as her sister's, though not as callused, Fargo noted.

While Harmony tended her sister and unloaded camping supplies from the wagon's box, Fargo rode off and shot a small mule deer. When he returned to the camp, Harmony was hammering the last stake of an old army tent she'd pitched in the pine shade.

"You two travel in style," Fargo commented, removing the field-dressed deer from the pinto's back.

The blonde gave the stake one more rap. "We found the tent in Papa's storage shed."

"Out here it's best to sleep under the stars. Or under a simple lean-to, if it looks like rain."

"Oh, and why is that?" Harmony said. "To show how tough we are?"

"To show how stupid you're *not*." Fargo was gathering rocks for a fire ring. "You've pitched your tent in the hunting grounds of both the northern Shoshone and the Utes. The Arapaho and the Cheyenne stay mostly on the Rockies' eastern slopes, but even they have been known to stray this way on occasion. None of those tribes is acting friendly to whites just now. And if they came upon two ladies like you and your sis . . . well, they might get some nasty ideas."

"I don't see what that has to do with our tent, Mr. Fargo," Charity said. The brunette had climbed inside and was poking her head out the door.

Fargo set a rock down with a grunt. "It's easier to conceal a lean-to than a tent, and it doesn't take near as long to strike a lean-to."

"Why don't you let us worry about that, Mr. Fargo?" said Charity with a haughty sneer. She turned to her sister. "Harmony, I'm going to lay down for a bit. My head is splitting."

"You let me know if you need anything, sis."

"Perhaps an extra pillow?"

"Right away."

When Harmony had brought Charity a feather pillow from the wagon, Harmony walked over to where Fargo crouched beside the fire he'd laid within the rocks and was skinning out the deer. She sat on a log to one side and regarded him wistfully.

"Where did you learn so much about camping and such, Mr. Fargo?"

"Here and there."

"You been on the frontier a long time?"

"Since I was knee-high to spit, I guess you could say."

Harmony folded her hands in her lap as Fargo deftly ran his Arkansas toothpick between the hide and skin of the limp mule deer, scraping as he went

17

to preserve as much meat as possible. "Charity and I were city girls before we joined Papa in the mining camp. Didn't get out much. Ma kept us busy, workin' in her establishment."

Fargo wasn't all that interested, but the girl obviously wanted to talk. "What kind of an establishment was that?"

"Uh." Harmony paused, looked at her hands. "A brothel."

Fargo snapped his head up. "Pshaw."

"Oh, don't misunderstand! Charity and I had nothing to do with hostessing. We were much too young, and Ma wouldn't have let us entertain the men at any age. We just did the cookin' and cleanin' and laundry and such."

Fargo returned to skinning. "How'd you end up with Three-Gun Pete in Heart's Desire?"

"Ma died from a water fever," Harmony said. "That's when Pa sent for us. He'd hung up his six-shooters by then and was calling himself LeFleur."

"And what do you and Charity call yourselves?"

"Ellis. That was my ma's name on her ma's side."

Fargo had laid the tenderloin across a long, flat rock, and was cutting the tender, red-brown meat into three-inch steaks to roast on sticks. "You and your sis are right complicated."

Harmony got up and strolled over to the wagon. "Would you like some coffee, Mr. Far—" She stopped suddenly and wheeled toward him. "Wait a minute. You're the one they call the Trailsman, aren't you?"

Fargo chuffed. "Been called a lot o' things."

"I should have recognized you. I've heard you described enough times."

Fargo turned to her and sleeved sweat from his brow. "Say again?"

"One of Ma's pleasure girls, Dame Elizabeth, talked about you all the time. Said you were the best . . ." Harmony let the rest of the sentence die on her lips as she favored him with a fresh, admiring stare. Her eyes pulsed like embers. "Well, you know."

"Dame Elizabeth," Fargo said, pausing in his work to stare off across the creek, remembering. "She worked for your ma?"

"The last year of Ma's life."

"How's dear Lizzy doin', anyway?"

"She ran off with a traveling playacting show," Harmony said. "I heard they were hit by Comanches north of Fort Worth. All were killed, their wagon burned."

"Damn, that's a shame," Fargo said, remembering the whore's many talents. "Well, I'll have a drink to Dame Elizabeth tonight."

"A drinkin' man," Harmony said with a devilish glint in her eye. "Maybe I'll have a shot of something myself." She glanced at the tent and, holding a hand to the side of her mouth, whispered, "Don't tell sis. She doesn't approve."

"But she worked in her father's saloon." Fargo snorted.

"She didn't have nothin' to do with drink slingin', just kept herself holed up with the account books in Papa's office," Harmony said, rummaging around in a gunnysack. "Charity's as straitlaced as the queen's corset."

As Harmony put coffee on to boil, Fargo gathered branches from a nearby aspen stand, sharpening the ends for roasting sticks. Fargo returned to the crackling fire, running a thumb across the point of a stick, and saw Harmony watching him from a flat rock. The devilish glint had returned to her eyes.

She turned away, flushing slightly, and rose. She threw her hands above her head in a catlike stretch, drawing the orange blouse taut against her firm, round breasts. Her honey blond curls hung straight down from the back of her head.

She lowered her arms with a sigh. "Think I'll go

take a dip in the creek, rid myself of that bounty-hunter filth. You think there's any pools nearby where a girl can get herself a good soak?" She rolled her head on her shoulders, as if working out the kinks.

"Try upstream," Fargo said. "But don't wander far. Like I said, this is—"

"Yeah, I know," Harmony said, rummaging around in a trunk beside the tent's buttoned flap, her pert butt facing the Trailsman. "This is Injun country. How could I forget?"

"Better eat somethin'."

"I'll eat when I get back." She glanced over her shoulder, touching a coquettish finger to her rich bottom lip. "Dame Elizabeth couldn't talk enough about you. Described you in detail, as a matter of fact."

She giggled and trotted off through the brush along the river.

Fargo looked after her. He chuckled to himself, then regarded the venison steaks laid out on the flat rock. They'd keep. He slid the coffeepot to one side of the fire. While the girl bathed, he might as well drag the dead bounty hunters away from the camp. The bodies would only attract predators after dark.

First, he'd best check on Miss Charity.

He strode over to the tent and opened his mouth to speak, but thought better of it. The girl might be sleeping. He edged the flap open. He peeked inside. His chest grew instantly tight, his breathing shallow.

Inside, Miss Charity reclined on a bed of multicolored quilts—naked as an Indian goddess. She lay curled on her left side, long, angular back and full, round butt facing Fargo. Her hair was piled atop her head, so that even her delicate neck was exposed. One foot rested on the other, the soles pink and clean, the toes curled under.

The girl owned skin the color of ivory, and it was every bit as smooth.

A half-moon of porcelain breast peeked out from beneath the slender arm folded across her chest.

The heat from inside the tent pushed against Fargo's face. The air smelled of canvas and perfumed woman. He blinked sweat from his brows as he watched a bead of perspiration slide over the curve of Charity's ass and drift slowly along the back of her thigh.

The girl drew a sudden deep breath, her back rising, and Fargo released the door flap and sleeved his brow.

He felt as though he'd been brained with a Ute war club.

Christ . . .

The image of the girl's naked back seared into his brain, Fargo headed out to the brushy meadow and began the tedious task of removing the bodies. One at a time, he dragged them across the wagon road and rolled them into a deep ravine. They'd make a tasty meal for some wolf or wandering griz'.

When he'd finished, he unsaddled and unbridled the hardcases' horses and turned them loose. Some rancher or prospector would be glad to find them and the tack Fargo piled under an aspen.

He strolled back to the camp to find the fire low, and no Harmony.

Christ . . .

Vexed, Fargo stomped off along the creek in the same direction the girl had gone.

"Took you long enough."

He turned toward the creek.

Harmony was resting her butt against a boulder in the middle of the chuckling stream. Her feet were in the water. She was as naked as her sister, but she was *facing* the Trailsman, a coy grin spreading across her mouth and sparkling in her eyes.

She held an elbow across her breasts. That hand lightly clutched her other arm. She lifted one knee to cover the blond triangle between her thighs and gave it a flirtatious wag, playing hide-and-seek.

"You're too far from the camp," Fargo said. "It ain't safe."

"You'll protect me." She laughed and kicked water. "You're the Trailsman."

While Harmony studied the brawny, bristle-cheeked man on the shore, grinning, he abruptly turned away, disappearing into the pine canopy. She frowned.

The water churned about her feet as she stared, bewildered, into the pines.

Had he gone? Hadn't he liked what he'd seen? Or were all those stories Elizabeth had told her nothing more than lies?

Maybe he didn't like girls at all. . . .

She'd become thoroughly crestfallen, when he reappeared wearing only his hat. Her heart turned somersaults and her thighs became water. She watched him stalk toward her, water spraying up around his sculpted thighs and jutting pole, and her heart pounded like summer thunder.

He marched fast, coming on like a storm, moving his arms as if to pull the creek back behind him. He had such a grim, purposeful look on his broad brown face that Harmony suddenly felt as though she were being pursued by an enraged grizzly.

His chin dropped, his hat brim pulled low over his eyes.

"Wait," she said, "hold on, now. . . . I . . ."

Fargo stopped before her. His broad, damp chest rose and fell, the massive shoulders rolling back, the pectorals tightening and showing veins through the saddle brown hide. "You what?"

"I never did this before. I—"

"Sure you have."

"Okay, I have, but"—she dropped her eyes—"but never with nothin' like *that*. Oh, God, you're hung like a *fence post*!"

"Never call a girl for a woman's work. . . ." Fargo started to turn away.

"No! Wait!"

She slid off the boulder and wrapped her arms around his neck. She kissed him long and hard, running her hands down his back and shoulders, digging her fingers in, feeling the edges of each well-defined muscle. Her tongue pushed and slid against his.

Fargo's shaft tightened, prodded the soft nap between her legs. Goose bumps rose on his arms as the girl probed and caressed, grunting, sighing, lifting each leg in turn, rubbing against his thighs as if she were somehow trying to climb *inside* him.

Against Fargo's callused hands, her skin was silky, damp, and cool. He ran both hands down the firm twin globes of her butt, then brought them back up, running his fingers through the crease. . . .

"Ohhh." She laughed, jerking as if chilled.

She pulled her lips from his, then lowered her head down his chest and belly, kissing, nibbling as she went. She knelt in the stream, taking the shaft in both hands, looking up at the throbbing purple head with the eyes of a girl who'd finally received the present she'd been begging for. When she lifted her gaze to his, smiling gleefully, her eyes slightly crossed, Fargo almost came in her hands.

"Can I . . . play with it?" she asked.

Fargo set his hat on the boulder. "It's all yours, honey."

She ran her hands up and down the shaft for a long, excruciating time before she finally closed her mouth over the head. She sucked it like a lollipop, breaking off occasionally to run her tongue down the long, curved length of the throbbing member. The Trailsman couldn't hear above the river's rush and murmur, but he could tell she was cooing and muttering.

When he couldn't take it anymore, Fargo pulled her to her feet. With ease, he lifted her in his bulging arms. She laughed and wrapped her legs around his back, as if they were about to play giddyap.

He lifted her still farther up his waist. Snaking his forearms under her thighs, he gently lowered her over the organ.

Her eyes flashed terror as her hair bobbed about her face. "Oh . . . no . . . I . . . Jesus . . . I *can't* . . . !"

He began to slide her back up toward the head. She clamped her hands down on his shoulders, digging her fingers in.

"No," she sobbed. "Let me stay."

He dropped her back down until he was fully inside her, feeling the hot, wet core of her expanding and contracting around him. She shuddered and dug her heels into his back. He lifted her, dropped her back down again.

"Oh, yes," she breathed, kissing his forehead and running her hands brusquely through his hair, pulling at his ears. "Oh, God, yes."

He held her there in his bulging arms, running her slender pink body up and down his shotgun-barrel organ, the river rippling against his calves, until he felt an explosion brewing at the base of his balls. He held her still against him, and, his hard jaw jutting, walked her toward the far side of the stream. She hung impaled against him, head bobbing, eyelids fluttering, her shallow breath catching in her throat.

He found a patch of ferns.

Staying inside her, he laid her back against the soft, cool plants. He rose up on his arms, pulled out of her, then thrust back in savagely. Her thighs spread as if she'd been cleaved in two.

"Ohhhh!" she cried.

She screamed and clubbed his shoulders with her fists. She tipped her head back and squeezed her eyes closed.

He grunted and tipped his head back, emptying his loins into her core.

4

The Trailsman and Harmony remained in the ferns for another half hour, frolicking like savages. It was Fargo who finally suggested, after he and the girl had made love for a third time, with Harmony straddling him, that they head back to the camp.

"Fire's probably out," Fargo said, heading for the stream.

The sun had fallen behind the western ridges. Cool purple shadows filled the basin while birds flitted to and fro about the still-bright sky.

"No, wait," Harmony begged, reaching for his finally spent member. "I don't wanna leave here . . . not *ever!*"

Fargo chuckled. "What would your sister say about that?"

"Oh, God—Charity!" Harmony leaped to her feet and followed Fargo into the river, where they both took a quick, cleansing dip in a pool.

Fargo grabbed his hat off the boulder, and he and the girl continued to the other side, where they hastily dressed before the girl scampered off to the camp.

Charity was sound asleep in the tent, unmolested by savages of any stripe. But the fire was a pile of gray ashes sending up a thin ribbon of pine smoke.

While Harmony dressed in the tent, Fargo began rebuilding the fire. Behind him, the Ovaro snorted. Fargo turned to the horse—black on both ends, white in the middle. The pinto lowered its head and stared at Fargo, mocking the man for another in a long line of indiscretions.

The damn horse must smell her on him. . . .

"Ah, shut up." Fargo grunted, breaking a pine branch over his knee.

The Trailsman and Harmony ate heartily, both of them going through the deer tenderloins like gandy dancers. Charity came out of the tent to only pick at her food, perform her "ablutions" in the weeds along the river, then bid Fargo and her sister a cordial goodnight. Her head was still hurting, but she was sure she'd feel better in the morning.

Fargo admired the girl's narrow-waisted, full-hipped figure as she retreated to the tent. He relished the side view of her large, conical breasts jouncing around behind her wrapper when she bent to open the tent's fly, her long auburn hair swirling down her back.

"Where you gonna sleep?" Harmony asked while they lolled about the fire later, their bellies full of venison, sipping hot coffee from tin cups. Fargo's Henry rifle was propped against a log to his right, fully loaded, a shell seated in the chamber.

"Right here."

Harmony sipped her coffee, then glanced at the tent behind her. She turned to Fargo with a frisky glint in her eye. She'd pulled her hair back in a ponytail. She had the serene flush of a satisfied woman. "Can we do it again?" she whispered, adding, "Later?"

"Nope."

She frowned. "How come?"

"It's full dark, and I have to keep my wits about me. You'd best sleep in the tent with sis. I'll be up roamin' around, wake you up."

"How come so cold all of a sudden?"

"Better cold this side of the sod than down below."

"Bastard!" She got up, tossed her coffee into the brush, and turned to the tent. Fargo watched her round ass, clad in denims now that the cold night had come down, disappear inside.

Fargo glanced at his horse, watching from the trees near the creek. "Was I talkin' to you?"

He leaned forward to fill his cup, then stood and, picking up his rifle, strolled about the camp, watching, listening, and sipping the joe. When he was satisfied that no enemies lurked, he glanced into the wagon box.

The coffin containing Three-Gun Pete LeFleur sat surrounded by crates and steamer trunks. The air around it was still tainted with the flowery aromas of spilled perfume.

Fargo snorted.

What he didn't get himself into . . .

He built up the fire and rolled into his soogan. He crossed his hands behind his head and lay staring up at the stars, his ears pricked to the night. A meteor flashed, trailing sparks to the western horizon. The Big Dipper loomed, the North Star flickering dully.

Behind him, the creek gurgled across its toothy bed.

After a time, a nightbird cooed, three regular cries, as if signaling another. Fargo lifted his head, lines carving into his forehead as he peered into the shadows beyond the fire.

As if in answer to the bird, a rustling sounded inside the tent.

Fargo turned his glance that way, saw the flap slide wide. Harmony's blond head poked out. The slender, pert-bosomed body followed. The girl stood before the tent, silhouetted against the pale canvas, her hair wisping in the night breeze. She wore a thin silvery gown, a cape thrown loosely about her shoulders.

The Trailsman sighed.

The girl moved toward him around the fire, lifting her bare feet with a dancer's grace. The fire winked in her hair like sequins.

She stood over him, smiling. Her chest rose and fell slowly. She opened the cape, then let it and her gown slide down her shoulders and flutter to the ground. Above the waist she was naked. Her small, round breasts stood proudly out from her chest, nipples jutting. Her body was relieved in umber firelight and velvet shadows.

Fargo's right eye slitted.

"Having a change of . . . heart?" she asked just above a whisper.

Throwing his blanket aside, the Trailsman scissored his left foot out savagely, cutting the girl's feet out from beneath her. As Harmony fell with an exasperated shriek, an arrow whistled through the air where her head had just been, burying its strap-iron tip in a pine behind Fargo. The wooden thump and vibrating shudder resounded in the hushed night.

Fargo rose to a sitting position, drawing his Colt .44 from the holster coiled around his saddle horn, thumbing back the trigger. A buckskin-clad Indian, feathers in his long greasy hair, stood on the other side of the fire, bow still raised, a surprised expression stretching his raw-boned, painted face.

Fargo fired twice. The Indian gave a guttural scream and tumbled back into the shadows on the other side of the fire, the bow and his long hair flying, arrows rattling in the quiver hanging between his shoulder blades.

A footfall sounded behind Fargo. Harmony screamed.

The Trailsman stood, turning, as another Ute brave leaped toward him, stone-headed war club raised high. Knowing he couldn't get a shot off fast enough, Fargo dropped the revolver and threw his arms up, his left hand wrapping around the wrist holding the club. As he stepped back, half turning, he snaked his right arm under the brave's free arm and flung himself straight back while kicking high with both feet.

After his back hit the ground, the Indian turned a somersault in the air over the Trailsman's head. Screaming and kicking his moccasined feet, the Ute hit the middle of the fire with a loud thump.

The coffeepot barked, and sparks flew.

The Indian, whose head had smacked a sharp rock, gave a single grunt and kicked a few times as the fire reignited around him, instantly filling the air with the stench of burning flesh and hair.

Harmony screamed.

Fargo followed her gaze toward the wagon, then threw himself to the right as two quick flashes appeared just off the wagon's tailgate.

Pop! Pop!

One of the slugs tore through the tent. The other smacked into a trunk near the tent's door flap.

Rolling off a shoulder, Fargo grabbed his .44 and came up firing. When his fourth shot had thundered, he squinted through the wafting powder smoke. Beyond the camp, a man's shadow jerked and bobbed, twigs snapping under running feet. Long hair flew as the Indian retreated across the open meadow.

Fargo grabbed his Henry and, leaping across the burning Indian's quivering feet, glanced at Harmony. "Check on your sister!"

Running toward the retreating Indian, he thumbed the Henry's hammer back. At the edge of the pines he stopped, raised the rifle to his shoulder, drew a bead on the leaping silhouette, and squeezed.

The rifle leaped and boomed.

"Ugghhh!"

Weeds snapped. A dull thud.

Fargo stared across the meadow. He didn't cotton to back-shooting, but the Indian, probably part of a small hunting party, might have alerted others.

He walked over to the squirming figure. Brown eyes turned up to him, starlight dancing in the irises. The young Ute, no older than fifteen, muttered several phrases while tears smeared his war paint.

Fargo savvied enough of the tongue to translate: "Put me out of my pain, you white bastard."

Fargo granted the young brave a merciful end. He cursed and strode back to the camp. Both women were outside the tent, Charity in a thin robe, looking around distastefully, while Harmony tried pulling the burning Indian from the fire by one moccasined foot.

"You all right?" he asked the brunette.

Eyes glazed, staring at the burning Ute, Charity only nodded.

"Here." Fargo nudged Harmony aside, took his rifle in his left hand, and gave the Indian a jerk with his right. The brave flew out of the fire, looking like a half-burned log but smelling like the devil's breakfast. The smoke and sparks wafted. Gagging and covering her mouth, Charity ran behind the tent.

Fargo turned to Harmony, who'd turned her own gaze to the arrow protruding from the pine trunk near the creek. Even in the shunting shadows, her face was drawn and pale.

"Have a change of heart?" Fargo asked.

No one slept much the rest of the night, least of all Fargo, who'd had three more bodies to get rid of.

At the first flush of dawn, he built up the fire for breakfast, set coffee to boil, and hitched the Ovaro to the wagon. The Ovaro was no puller—a fact that the stallion communicated to Fargo by raising its head haughtily as the Trailsman strapped it up—but it wouldn't go "hitch crazy" as some saddle horses did when they felt the weight of the wheeled contraption pulling the collar taut to its neck.

The Trailsman had carefully trained the horse for virtually any frontier situation.

"Mr. Fargo," Harmony said when they were on the trail later that morning, the sun glistening in the Ovaro's magnificent black-and-white coat, "Charity and I were talking earlier, and we decided to offer you the job."

The Trailsman turned to her. "The job?"

"Yes." The blonde beamed as if she'd just offered the stable boy the esteemed position of polishing the king's throne. "The job of guiding Charity and me—and Papa, of course—to Del Norte."

"You do seem capable enough," Charity said.

The brunette rode in the box behind Fargo and Harmony. She'd arranged a cozy nest for herself beside her father's coffin, complete with multiple quilts and several pillows. She'd even beseeched Fargo to rig a powder-blue parasol to the wagon's side panel, bathing her in cool purple shade.

Chisk, chisk, chisk, came the sound of her nail file.

"I don't know what to say, ladies," Fargo said, squinting over the pinto's bobbing head at the trail rising like tan ribbon over the sagebrush-carpeted hills. "That's quite an honor. Unfortunately, I'm going to have to turn you down."

"Turn us down?" Harmony said, frowning at him, looking hurt. "But why?"

"We'll certainly pay you for your time, Mr. Fargo," said Charity. "Does five hundred dollars sound reasonable?"

"I reckon five hundred would be a fair amount," Fargo said, moving easily with the wagon's bounce and sway, "but I don't take money to murder folks. Especially a couple of dunderheaded *women*folk. If I agreed to guide you and Three-Gun Pete to Del Norte—with that ten-thousand-dollar bounty on his bones—that's just what I'd be doin'."

The nail file's *chisk-chisk-chisk* suddenly stopped. "Please explain, Mr. Fargo."

"Two beautiful women slow-wheelin' around this

country in a beat-up buckboard, haulin' their old man's carcass to a town a good three days from here would be certain suicide even *if* their old man's carcass *wasn't* worth ten thousand dollars. An accomplice in such a suicidal endeavor would be committing murder."

"But you'd be *protecting* us!" said Harmony. "Just like you did yesterday and last night."

"You'd help us travel to Del Norte *safely*," chimed in Charity, albeit with less exuberance than her sister.

Fargo shook his head. "You'll have more bounty hunters on your trail than wolves on a calf crop. Sorry, ladies. You'd best bury your old man under a nice shade tree somewhere . . . anywhere." Fargo looked off, lifting a hand to shade his eyes from the sun. "How 'bout that big cottonwood yonder? Pretty view of the valley from there. Nice, peaceful place for Three-Gun's final rest."

"Papa's last wish was to be buried in Del Norte with Uncle Karl," said Harmony. "And that's where we intend to bury him."

Fargo looked over his shoulder at Charity.

"We have no choice," she said resolutely.

"Ladies," Fargo said, "I doubt your old man, if he really thought about the danger he was putting you in, would have wanted you to go through with this. I bet he'd think that big cottonwood yonder was as good a place as any . . . under the circumstances."

Both women regarded him coldly, and Charity said, "Thank you for the advice, Mr. Fargo. When we get to the next town, we'll take your leave."

Fargo shrugged. "Your funeral." He shook the reins over the pinto's back.

They continued along the trail in silence, both women giving Fargo the silent treatment. The Trailsman feigned chagrin, which, he'd learned from sundry past experiences with other piss-burned females, was a surefire way to keep the chattering down.

He built a cigarette and enjoyed the peace and quiet. Most likely, when these two beauties got to Jackpot, the little crossroads town about ten miles ahead, they'd realize the error of their ways and bury Three-Gun Pete in the burg's boothill cemetery, and take the stage back to where they came from.

If they had half as much sense as they did looks, that was. If not . . . well, Fargo wanted nothing to do with their demise. He was only one man, and his Henry repeater held only sixteen rounds. . . .

5

When they got to Jackpot, Charity very crisply directed Fargo to pull the wagon up to the town's single livery barn. The Trailsman did as he was told, set the brake, and jumped down from the driver's box. When he offered a hand to the women, both turned him a cold shoulder and crawled out of the wagon under their own power, haughtily fluffing the trail dust from their hair and gently flogging their skirts.

Fargo shrugged, grabbed his gear from the wagon box, unharnessed the pinto, and began moseying up the street.

"Skye?"

Fargo turned, puffing the stubby cigarette wedged in one corner of his mouth, his saddle and saddlebags perched on his left shoulder, his rifle boot and reins in his right hand. Harmony stared after him, pouting. Charity had gone into the livery barn to see about securing a mule.

"Where are you going?" the blonde inquired, her brows deeply ridged, red lips pooched out.

"Where I always go when I visit Jackpot." He jerked his chin up the street to a large two-story house painted pink and with a large shingle over its broad front porch announcing: MISS KATE'S PLEASURE EMPO-RIUM. The shingle below the main sign read: GIRLS AND MORE GIRLS! SATISFACTION GUARANTEED!

Reading the signs, the blonde dropped her jaw. She returned her blue eyes to his. "After . . . what we did . . . ?"

"That was yesterday," said Fargo with a roguish wink. "This is today." He turned and took three steps before stopping and turning back. "You change your mind about your crazy trek to Del Norte, I'll be glad to lend a shovel."

He winked again and continued up the street, winding through the heavy midday traffic. Not long later, he was perched at a table in the front window of Kate's saloon, quiet this time of the day, most of the girls upstairs sleeping off last night. His gear piled on a chair to his right, Fargo nursed a beer and surveyed the street.

The window was so dusty and fly-splattered that the Trailsman couldn't see much beyond a blur of pros-pectors' wagons bouncing along the street and scat-tered pedestrians moving along both boardwalks. From here, he had a good view of the livery stable, however. The wagon of the two fillies from Heart's Desire was parked between the barn's open doors, a tarp concealing the coffin.

Twirling her parasol, Charity stood just inside the barn's shadows, talking with a stoop-shouldered man with thick red hair and a mustache. They both re-garded the wagon. Still talking, Charity turned and followed the man into the barn. Meanwhile, Harmony, who'd been rummaging around amidst the gunnysacks piled on the street side of the wagon, grabbed one, turned, and strolled two doors down to the Booney Griggs Mercantile.

When Harmony had been in the store for several minutes, Charity and the red-haired hostler emerged from the barn's shadows. The hostler led out into the sunshine a big black gelding with white-socked front legs and a white spot on its left rear hip.

As the hostler backed the mule to the wagon, Fargo sipped his beer, running his appraising eyes across the big animal, noting the head-erect stance, well-defined hips, straight legs, and broad chest denoting strength and staying power.

Charity knew her mules. Too bad she didn't have some horse sense. Fargo had figured that soon after he'd lit a shuck, she and her sister would think seriously about the bounty hunters and Indians who'd attacked them, and forgo the expedition. They'd turn Three-Gun Pete shovel-down on the low hill overlooking the town, where gravestone tilted amidst the wild mahogany, sage, and one spindly cottonwood, and hop the next stage to civilization.

But there Charity stood, twirling her parasol and shrewdly appraising the hostler's work buckling the broad-chested mule to the wagon, while her sister brokered trail goods at the mercantile.

The Trailsman drained his beer and set the schooner down with more force than necessary.

They still intended to go through with their crazy mission.

Ornery damn females . . .

He ordered another beer. He'd give the girls more time to come to their senses on their own. But he was half finished with the second schooner when both women had climbed back aboard the wagon. Harmony sat down in the driver's seat, while Charity alit beside her, throwing her rich auburn hair out from the collar of her burgundy traveling cloak and raising the parasol above her head. Harmony flicked the reins against the mule's back, and the wagon pulled out into the street, between a Pittsburg ore wagon and a lumber dray.

Fargo puffed the cigarette he'd built, chewed the end, working tobacco flecks on his tongue with consternation. "Damn their fool hides," he told himself aloud, chewing the quirley. "Oh, well. They're full-growed, and I ain't their pa."

He sat back in his chair with a fatalistic sigh. He lifted his beer glass to his lips. Glancing through the streaked window toward the livery barn, he stopped the motion, then pulled the glass back down to the table.

The red-haired liveryman had stepped out from between the barn's open doors. He peered thoughtfully up the street, in the direction that the girls had taken out of town.

The man stood there for a time, worrying his thick mustache with the thumb and index fingers of his right hand. Then he strode across the street and out of Fargo's field of vision, no doubt entering one of the shops or saloons to Fargo's left.

Fargo leaned forward to see back along his side of the street, but couldn't see farther than two or three doors down. He leaned back in his chair and studied his beer with ridged brows, flicking his thumbnail against the beveled glass.

Minutes passed. Customers came and went around Fargo, who barely noticed, as his attention was riveted on the street. He hadn't taken another sip from his beer when his gaze went to three men mounting horses a half block away on his left. The trio, dressed in the homespun attire of poor stockmen, moved hastily, enervated looks on their sun-blistered faces beneath the brims of their weathered stockmen's hats.

Fargo watched closely as the men reined away from the boardwalk, angled their stock ponies into the street, and trotted past the whorehouse saloon in the direction Harmony and Charity had taken. Rifles were snugged down in their saddle sheaths, and holstered six-shooters flopped on their thighs. Their horses snorted, hooves thudding.

"Melvin, get that damn rattle-cart outta my way, damn ye!" one of the riders berated a slow-moving wagoner.

As the two horsemen swerved around the hay wagon, hoorahing their mounts and kicking up dust, the slow-moving wagoner stretched his arm high above his head and raised his middle finger.

When the two riders had disappeared to the Trailsman's right, dust sifting behind them, Fargo looked eastward along the street. The liveryman was crossing back over toward the livery barn, striding quickly and casting anxious glances after the harried horsebackers.

Fargo watched the man's slumped shoulders and bowed back disappear into the livery barn.

Fargo grunted. "You son of a bitch."

He removed his feet from the chair across from him, kicking the chair against the opposite wall. He tossed back his beer, kicked his own chair back, and stood. He grumbled a curse, tossed coins onto the table, and turned toward the door.

His way was blocked by a stout, broad-shouldered man in a floppy-brimmed black hat and red-checked shirt standing before him. The bearded but baby-faced man grinned a gap-toothed grin, raised a big Sharps rifle, and slung it butt-first toward Fargo.

The brass butt moved so quickly toward Fargo's head that the Trailsman had time to do little but flinch.

He heard the boom of his body hitting the floor before his lights flickered out like a wind-gusted lantern.

"Oh, darn!" Harmony said, pulling back on the mule's reins three miles south of Jackpot. "I think I should have taken that other trail back yonder."

"What other trail?" asked Charity, lowering the illustrated newspaper she'd been reading in the shade of her parasol. "I didn't see another trail."

"There was a narrow one to the left, about fifteen

miles out of town." Harmony reached into the carpetbag at her feet and hauled out a large quartered sheet of brown butcher paper.

She unfolded the paper—a map that one of her father's old mountain-man friends in Heart's Desire had drawn—and spread it out on her knees. She placed her finger on a spot on the stained paper and turned to her sister. "I think this is the one right here. Harold said we should take this little trail here and skirt the mountains. He felt that one would be the most sheltered and, you know, safer."

Charity leaned close to her sister and bowed her head to study the map. "Well, if we take that one, won't we . . . ?" She let her voice trail off as she squinted down at all the squiggly lines tracing trails, creeks, and rivers, and the large V shapes demarking mountains. "Oh, heck, this is rather complicated, isn't it?"

"Charity," Harmony said, a slight trill in her voice, "do you have any regrets about this? I mean, as we saw yesterday and last night, this *is* dangerous country. And we no longer have the Trailsman watching our backsides—"

The brunette snapped her head up, cutting her sister off. "We don't need the Trailsman—or *any* man, for that matter—watching our backsides. True, we've had a run of bad luck, but as long as we follow Harold's map and avoid these settlements he's marked with little skulls and crossbones, we should do just fine."

She plucked the map off Harmony's knees, holding it close to her face. "The Trailsman, indeed! What a scoundrel! Let me see. Hmmmm. It looks to me like if we continue the way we're going, we can take this trail here back east for a couple of miles, and catch the trail we missed right *here*."

The sound of pounding hooves rose to the women's ears. Both turned to see three riders galloping toward them.

"Oh, dear," muttered Charity.

"Not again," said Harmony, reaching down to fish around inside the carpetbag. She withdrew a small, silver-plated pocket pistol with ivory grips, and slid it between her rump and the seat back.

"What should we do?" Charity asked.

"We know we can't outrun 'em," Harmony said as the three riders approached, checking their dusty mounts down to trots. "I reckon we just sit tight. Maybe they'll ride on past."

The three riders—two average-sized men, and one big man in a red-checked shirt and black floppy-brimmed hat—shuttled glances between themselves and the girls. The big man's baby face sported a thin brown beard, and his blue eyes twinkled across the girls as though they were twin hunks of dried apricot pie buried in fresh whipped cream.

"Guess they're not gonna pass," Harmony said, crestfallen, muttering the words through taut lips.

"Hello, ladies," said the man riding up on their left as the big man and the other man halted their horses to the wagon's right. "How're you two doin' today?"

His long, greasy black hair fell straight down from his blue derby hat, the crown of which was encircled by a rawhide string of long, sharp animal teeth.

Harmony said, "Just fine, thanks."

Charity offered a wooden smile.

The biggest of the three leaned out from his horse to peer into the wagon bed. "Anything we can, uh . . . help ya with?"

"We're just stopping to give the mule a breather," said Charity. "But thanks for asking."

"Shucks, that's no problem," said the third rider, a blond young man with buckteeth and a funnel-brimmed hat. Since his chin was little more than a blunt knob, the hat's chin thong had run up beneath his lower lip, giving him a preposterous look. "Me and my brothers—Big Roy Luther there, and Milton, otherwise known as Dawg—we're always willin' to help a couple pretty ladies in times of trouble."

"Well, as you can see," said Harmony, releasing the wagon's brake and flicking the reins over the mule's back, "we don't need any help. Love to stay and chat, but we'd best get on back to the ranch with these supplies."

"Yes," said Charity, nervously rolling her eyes from rider to rider, her hair bobbing as the wagon bounced forward, "we wouldn't want to keep our father or our brother, the Santo Domingo Kid, waiting."

Harmony slid her sister a dubious look. Charity shrugged a shoulder.

"The Santo Domingo Kid, eh?" said the big man, Roy Luther, laughing. "Dang, don't he sound tough? I bet he chews up nails and spits out tacks!"

The three firebrands roared. The one with the chin-strap under his lip swung his right leg over his saddle horn and leaped into the wagon box.

"Hey, what do you think you're doing?" exclaimed Harmony.

6

As the firebrand chuckled and stretched his arms to maintain his balance, he gigged his gray mare ahead. He reached down and grabbed the mule's halter, then hauled back on the reins.

The mule took several more plodding steps, braying and flicking its ears angrily, and finally brought itself to a halting stop in the brush to the right of the trail.

As if in protest, the big beast lifted its snout high and brayed as loud as a Viking horn.

"Goddamn you!" exclaimed Harmony, shuttling her enraged gaze from man to man. "We done told you we gotta be on our way. You got no right to stop us!"

"Oh, sure we do," said the man called Dawg, riding up close to the driver's box, running his shiny black eyes across Charity's well-filled blouse. "You two done got somethin' we *want*."

"Found it!" yelled the blond man in the wagon box. "The coffin's right here under the tarp!"

Heart pounding, Harmony reached behind her back to grab the pocket pistol. It had slid toward the outside of the seat, and she twisted around to grab it with her right hand. As she hauled it out from behind her,

Dawg leaped off his horse, landing in the driver's box before Charity.

Harmony aimed the pistol at him, thumbing the hammer back. Before she could squeeze the trigger, he grabbed her wrist. She jerked it free. As he grabbed it again, she squeezed the trigger.

The report was little louder than a twig snapping.

Dawg's bark drowned out the shot's echo. "Ahh!"

He jerked the gun from Harmony's grip with one hand while covering his cheek and ear with the other. "You *bitch*!"

"What happened?" asked Roy Luther, still sitting the mare beside the mule, holding his long-barreled S & W chest-high in his right hand.

"She shot me, the little bitch!" Dawg removed his hand from his cheek, revealing a slender blood streak traveling from just above the right corner of his mouth to his ear, the lobe of which was gone. Only a ragged, bloody stump remained.

"That was a pistol shot?" Roy Luther laughed. "I thought that was you breakin' wind."

Dawg glared down at Harmony. "God*damn* you!"

He slapped Harmony several times, quickly. When she raised her arms to protect herself, he slapped her arms and shoulders.

"No! Stop it!" Charity cried.

Harmony peeked out from between her wrists. "That's what you get for foolin' with us, you bastard!"

"Foolin' with you, huh?" Dawg drew his Colt, aiming it at Harmony's head. "How 'bout if I drill a bullet through your goddamn head? How would you like that kinda foolin'?"

"Stop it!" Charity screamed, pushing herself to her feet and beating the firebrand's left shoulder with both fists. Dawg knocked her back down with an elbow and, jabbing the barrel toward Harmony, thumbed his revolver's hammer back.

The girl lowered her head to her knees and squeezed her eyes closed. "Leave me be, you bastard!"

"Yeah, leave 'em be, Dawg," said the blond cutthroat in the wagon box. "Christ almighty, don't kill that girl. Look at her. Once we get the bounty on ol' Three-Gun here, we can keep these girls for wives, and have us all kinds of fun!"

Dawg cursed and rammed his Colt's barrel hard against Harmony's head. "Look what she done to my face, Burt!"

"Ah, it's just a scratch, ye Nancy-boy." Burt stared into the coffin and whistled. "Sure as shootin'—here lies Three-Gun Pete LeFleur. Looks just like his picture on the wanted dodger." Eyes aglow, he shuttled his gaze between Dawg and Roy Luther. "Ain't Pa gonna be pleased?"

"You sure it's him?" asked Roy Luther, still holding the mule's halter.

"Pa'll know for sure," Dawg said, clasping his neckerchief tight to his bloody face and ear. "He claims he seen Three-Gun Pete in Abilene one time, when Pete and four other gents was robbin' a mercantile."

"Father never robbed a mercantile," Charity intoned with a haughty gasp. "Only banks owned by Yankees."

"Shut up!" Dawg ordered, halfheartedly swinging Harmony's pocket pistol at her. He turned to Burt. "Slide that lid back on the coffin and get me some rope I can tie these two up with. I don't trust neither of 'em further than I could throw 'em into a stiff wind."

He stomped his boot down hard on the floor of the driver's box and glared at the blonde. "*Damn*, my face burns like holy hell!"

Roy Luther had ridden his horse up to Harmony's side of the wagon, and scowled up at Dawg. "Git down from there, and git yourself cleaned up. I'll take

it from here. Oughta be ashamed of yourself, actin'
like a damn whipped dog around ladies."

"Ladies?" said Dawg. "Bullshit!"

As Roy Luther swung heavily down from his saddle,
Dawg cuffed Harmony once more, then climbed awk-
wardly down from the wagon and tramped out into
the rocks and brush, toward a gurgling run-out spring.
Roy Luther swung his extended pistol from Harmony
to Charity and back again, and thumbed the hammer back.

"Now I want no more nonsense outta you two, or,
pretty as you are, I'm gonna fill you so full of hot lead
you won't hold a thimbleful of water." He raised his
high-pitched, childlike voice, and squinted his tiny
eyes. "Understand?"

The women glared at him, but fear shone in their
eyes. Smiling with self-satisfaction, Roy Luther kept
his pistol aimed at the women and slipped his lariat
from his saddle horn. He tossed the coiled rope up to
Burt, who'd slid the lid back onto the coffin and replaced the tarp, and was standing in the wagon box
behind and between the ladies.

"Tie 'em both with that," Roy Luther said. "Tie
their hands and feet. They make one move on you,
I'm gonna shoot 'em." He nodded and rose up on the
balls of his feet, puffing out his chest. "If there's one
thing I don't cotton to, it's sassy women."

"As if you've had experience with *any* kind of
woman!" snapped Harmony, jutting her chin at the
big, baby-faced man.

"See now?" said Roy Luther through clenched
teeth. "That's just the sorta thing I was talkin' about."

Cutting two-foot lengths of rawhide from the lariat,
Burt laughed. "Shit, these two can make any kind of
move on me they want. This is a fine coupla fillies!
Me, I want the blonde."

He gave Harmony a quick peck on the cheek. She
winced with revulsion, and jerked her face away.

"I like 'em with a little piss and vinegar," Burt added, chuckling.

"Shut up and get to work, little brother." Roy Luther glanced over his right shoulder to where Dawg knelt in the rocks bathing his cheek and ear at the spring. "I'm hungry. And we best get that dead pistoleer to the ranch before any more bounty hunters show up. These two no doubt been trailing bounty trackers like shit trails blowflies."

Burt roughly jerked Harmony's hands behind her back and began looping the rope around her wrists. "What about that big hombre in buckskins the liveryman said these two rode into town with?"

Roy Luther threw his head back, cackling. "Hell, he won't know what day it is fer a month of Sundays. I laid him out cold!"

Wincing as Burt tied her wrists, Harmony glanced darkly at Charity, who heaved a fatalistic sigh.

Roy Luther saw the looks on the women's faces, and whooped with glee. "That's right, ladies. That big fella ain't even gonna remember his own name before we done collected the bounty money for Three-Gun Pete. And then, heck, you'll have done got yourselves hitched!"

"You won't get away with this," Charity said, wincing as Burt tied her ankles. "Our father is *not* your property. We promised to bury him in the place he specified, and that's what we intend to do."

"No, you ain't, honey-girl." Burt chortled, jerking Charity over the seat and into the freight box. He brushed his cheek lustfully against hers as he shoved her down to her knees. "Your trail done stopped right here, and your old man's gonna make us rich!"

When Burt had gotten Harmony seated beside her sister, Roy Luther holstered his pistol, mounted his mare, and turned toward the spring. "Come on, blame it, Dawg. You ain't got all day to fool with that scratch."

"It's more than a scratch, damn it!" barked Dawg, stalking toward the wagon holding his wet neckerchief to his cheek and ear, his wet, black hair dancing about his long hawkish face. "That bitch damn near blew my head off!"

Dawg threatened Harmony. Harmony threatened Dawg. Roy Luther and Burt intervened and, finally, Burt slapped the reins against the mule's back, and the wagon rolled off into the sage on the right side of the trail.

Roy Luther led the way atop his gray mare. Dawg followed, scowling over his horse's head at Harmony and Charity and clutching his neckerchief to his face.

The wagon clattered cross-country, at times slamming so viciously over eroded gullies and hummocks that the two girls, bouncing around like jelly beans in a near-empty jar, yelled and cried, berating the driver. When they'd turned onto a trace only somewhat smoother than the cross-country dogleg they'd taken, Harmony found herself staring longingly through the dust of the wagon's wheels, beyond Dawg's plodding dun, at their backtrail.

"Looking for your night in shining armor?"

Bouncing around beside Harmony, Charity regarded her blond sister with faint mocking in her eyes. Harmony turned the corners of her mouth down, and dropped her gaze with chagrin.

"Turns out your Trailsman wasn't so tough, after all," Charity jibed.

"These rannies must've bushwacked him," Harmony said, turning her head to squint, hard jawed, at Roy Luther riding ahead of the wagon. "That fatso couldn't have taken Skye down in a fair fight."

"Skye?" Charity regarded her sister, befuddled. Understanding came to her eyes, and she rested her head on Harmony's shoulder. "I didn't realize what a shine you'd taken, Harmony. I'm sorry."

"It's okay." The blonde brushed her cheek against

47

her sister's temple. "It doesn't matter, anyway. These fools didn't realize that Skye—I mean, the *Trailsman*—had cut out on us." She looked again at their backtrail. "I do hope he's all right, though."

Charity turned her dour gaze to the coffin bouncing before her bound feet. "It's Papa I'm worried about." Lifting her gaze to Dawg scowling at them from his dun's saddle, she added, "And us . . ."

Ten minutes later, the wagon climbed a low bench and rolled into the yard of a small ramshackle ranch consisting of a plank-board cabin and barn and two falling-down corrals. A few skinny cows peppered the brown pastures surrounding the place, and dusty red chickens clucked in the yard.

Several screamed as the wagon turned around a rain barrel and pulled to a stop before the small roofless porch fronting the cabin. A thin smoke ribbon trailed from the tin chimney pipe.

"Pa!" Roy Luther shouted. "Come on out and see what your sons brought home!"

He swung down from the mare too fast for his weight. He stumbled, dropped to a knee, pushed himself back to his feet, and jogged toward the cabin. He'd just mounted the rotting wood porch when the front door creaked open, and a short, gray-bearded man stepped out, his thin hair mussed, his eyes red.

"What the hell's all the ruckus about?" came the throaty grumble as the old man sleepily smacked his lips and batted his eyes.

Grinning with pride, Roy Luther threw his arm out to indicate the wagon. Dust billowed on the late-afternoon breeze, and the mule gave another bray.

"What the hell you bring a wagon home fer?" The old man looked around the yard. "Where's my seed bulls? I send you boys to town for seed bulls, and you bring me back an *old wagon*?"

"Ha, ha!" Roy Luther laughed. "We done forgot

about the seed bulls, Pa, but how 'bout a coupla seed *bitches*?" Roy Luther was so thrilled with himself that he laughed again and slapped his hands down on the side of the wagon box, making both girls jerk with alarm.

"And they're just the cherry on top, Pa!" said Burt, who'd leaped into the wagon box and was sliding the tarp back toward the end gate. "Yes, sir, you ain't seen nothin' yet!"

Roy Luther and Dawg stood around the wagon, their father standing back near the porch, a skeptical look on his deeply lined face. Burt pried the lid off the coffin and stepped back like a magician showing the rabbit in his hat. The old man lifted his head a little to peer into the coffin. He pressed his lips together, squinting his eyes distastefully.

"What in the hell kinda foul business you boys been up to?" He glanced at the girls still sitting with their backs to the driver's box, dusty and silent, eyes dark with fear and anger. "And who in the hell's these females?"

"This here is Three-Gun Pete LeFleur," Burt crowed. He glanced at the girls. "And these're his daughters. They was takin' their pa to be buried, and we swooped down on 'em like forty hawks on a sittin' quail!"

The old man's right cheek twitched. As if to himself, he whispered, "Three-Gun Pete LeFleur . . ."

"The old pistoleer," Roy Luther said.

"Have a look, Pa." Burt had fished the wanted dodger out of his pants pocket. He held it out over the wagon box, where the evening breeze snatched at it, threatening to tear it away.

Slowly, as if still suspecting his boys had gotten drunk, or worse, the old man stepped forward and took the paper. He gazed down at it for a moment, running his hooded eyes across the picture and moving his lips, sounding out the few words he recognized. His face flushing and his eyes brightening slightly, he stretched his gaze again to the coffin.

Louder this time: "Three-Gun Pete LeFleur . . ."

Before anyone could say anything, he threw an arm out toward Roy Luther. "Help me up." Roy Luther helped the old man climb the wheel spokes, then step over the side of the box and into the wagon.

Stumbling and throwing his arms out for balance, the old man maneuvered through the trunks and gunnysacks to the coffin, planted a gnarled hand on the box's right side, and stooped close for a good look at the corpse's face. He straightened as much as his creaky spine would allow, his gray beard balling with a grin, revealing three or four teeth remaining in his black gums.

"It's him, all right. I recognize the old coot, but what the hell? How . . . ?"

Burt said, "Red Mitchell over to the livery barn heard he'd been shot. There was a rumor his two daughters had hauled him away from Heart's Desire to bury him down south somewheres. So, when this here wagon and these two fine-lookin' fillies roll up to his livery barn lookin' for a mule, he sneaks a peak into the coffin."

"He compared the face to the one on an old wanted dodger he had in his office," added Roy Luther. "And found himself holdin' a royal flush."

"Only," Burt said, "bein' a peaceable man, and wantin' no truck with the big hombre the girls was with at the time, he came and told us about it."

Dawg was bathing his ear at the stock trough before the house. "And about the ten-thousand-dollar reeward for the old bastard, dead or alive."

"And Red said it's still good," said Burt, breathless with excitement. "The ree-ward, I mean. It's offered by some express outfit back east. All we have to do is git the carcass to the sheriff over to the county seat, sign a paper sayin' we took down ol' Three-Gun our own selves, and he'll send our claim to the express company." Burt's eyes lit up. *"Ten thousand dollars!"*

"Ten thousand dollars," the old man muttered, tugging on his beard, looking even more befuddled than before. He leaned back against the coffin as if about to faint. "How can that be?"

Roy Luther laughed his high-pitched, cackling laugh. "Well, first thing tomorrow, Pa, when we drive old Three-Gun to the sheriff, we'll show ya!" He laughed louder and turned to the girls. "And looky here. Ain't these two a sight for sore eyes?"

The old man's bewildered glance fell on the girls, and his rheumy eyes sharpened. "Christ almighty. Those're the two that was drivin' this wagon? Those are Three-Gun's daughters?"

"Sure as shit," Burt said. "What do ya think—can we marry up with 'em? *Look* at 'em."

"We can't let 'em go," Roy Luther said. "They'll tell the sheriff we didn't kill ol' Three-Gun ourselves, and he'll want the money back."

The girls had been so worn down from the wagon ride, and so horrified by the four foul-smelling, evil-looking men before them, that they hadn't been able to formulate any words. Now, however, though she'd seen no one except the ranchers since leaving Jackpot, Charity threw her head back and screamed, "Help! Someone help us!"

The men looked at her, bemused, until she'd screamed herself out and dropped her head, sobbing. Beside her, Harmony's own face crumpled, and tears rolled down her cheeks.

"I'd say they're both pretty as speckled pups," observed the old man, running his own lusty gaze across the girls' womanly bodies, "but they're a mite hysterical. I couldn't get used to screamin' like that."

"They'll run down in no time, Pa," said Burt. "Soon as we put 'em to work."

"What do you say, Pa?" asked Roy Luther. "I want the blonde. Burt can have the dark-headed one."

"Hey, what about me?" said Dawg, turning from the stock trough with his ragged ear and furrowed cheek, his dark eyes snapping angrily. "That damn blonde shot my ear off!"

"Oh, she didn't shoot your ear off, Dawg," said Burt. "She just burned ya a little. And even if she did shoot your ear off, I don't see how it would figure into you marryin' her!"

"Yeah." Roy Luther laughed. "I don't think you two exac'ly started off on the right foot!"

The big man and Burt shared a guffaw.

Dawg stepped between them and reached into the wagon box, grabbed Harmony's arm, and began pulling her out of the box. "This one here's mine, and I'm takin' her right *now*!"

Before Harmony knew it, she found herself on the ground beside the wagon, looking up at Dawg's dark, enraged eyes. His lips stretched an angry grin as he grabbed her ankle and began dragging her across the yard. "You boys want me, I'll be in the barn," he called over his shoulder.

Dawg and Harmony didn't make it halfway across the yard before both Roy Luther and Burt wrestled their dark-haired brother to the ground. Scrambling to his knees, Dawg shouted, "Git your hands off me, brothers, or so help me—"

Burt dove atop him, slamming his back to the ground. Cursing, blood splashing from his cheek and ear, Dawg rolled Burt beneath him and began pummeling Burt's face with his fists.

Harmony had been thrown to the ground in the initial onslaught, and was now scooting away from the fighters on her butt, wincing as Roy Luther planted the toe of his right boot savagely against Dawg's ribs. Roy Luther was about to deliver another blow when the old man ran in, waving his hat and cursing his boys for fools.

As Burt and Roy Luther stood with their fists balled, staring down at the fallen Dawg, their faces crimson with exasperation, the old man picked up Burt's hat and whipped it at each one in turn, shouting, "Mine is a Christian house, and there will be no fornicating with Three-Gun's daughters until you're properly married to 'em. You boys *comprende* my lingo, or do I need to get the paddle?"

The sons stood down, relaxing their fists and dropping their chins with chagrin. "I reckon we understand, Pa," muttered Roy Luther.

"But there's only two girls," Burt pointed out, his right eye already beginning to swell. "How we gonna decide which two of us gets to marry 'em up?"

"Fairest way possible," barked the old man. "By drawin' straws. Then, when we done took Three-Gun Pete into Carlysle and collected the reward money, we'll fetch the preacher for a proper weddin'."

When Dawg began to grumble again about his ear and that he was due some satisfaction from the blonde, the old man swatted his good cheek with Burt's hat. Dawg lowered his head to his hands, blinking the sting from his eyes as the old man said, "Then—and only then—will fornication be allowed. In the meantime, we'll keep the girls locked up in the kitchen.

"Is that clear as rain to you dunderheads?" the old man shouted, the three sons standing, dusty and bruised, in a semicircle around him. Hanging their heads with chagrin, Roy Luther, Burt, and Dawg each nodded their agreement, and, spitting dust from their lips, muttered apologies.

"Now haul these women into the cabin," ordered the old man. "And let's see if they can cook!"

7

The long night passed slowly—more slowly for the girls than the men, though the old man made sure there was no "funny business." The girls slept in the kitchen after they were done cooking and cleaning up, and after supper and a couple games of cribbage, the "boys" were sent to their second-story bedroom and warned not to show their faces downstairs till dawn.

The next morning, the sun hadn't yet lifted its pink ball above the snow-mantled Mount Belford in the Sawatch Range east of the ranch before the cabin door squawked open and the old man stepped out. He yawned, stretching his galluses over his curved shoulders, and headed for the barn.

"Come on, boys, lead 'em on out," he called over his shoulder. "We'll tie 'em in the barn till we get back. Less chance of 'em gettin' away from there than the cabin."

Big Roy Luther stumbled over the threshold and onto the rotten porch, making the floorboards bark and squeak. He tugged on Harmony's arm, pulling her after him as he followed his father. He wrapped his arm around her shoulders and kissed her cheek.

"Come on, honey bunch. This is our big day. Ain't you excited?"

"Keep your goddamn smelly body away from me."

"Now, that ain't no way to talk to your soon-to-be husband."

"I ain't marryin' you, you son of a bitch!"

Roy Luther laughed and tugged her along. Wearing the same dress she'd been wearing yesterday, her hair hanging down over her drawn face, Harmony stumbled wearily along behind him. She felt beaten down to fine powder.

"Sure 'nough you are," said the big man. "I cain't wait, and I ain't just talkin' about your good cookin' neither. My balls are pure-dee tinglin' with the prospect of us sharin' our weddin' bed fer the first time!" Roy Luther stopped, threw his shaggy head back on his shoulders, and loosed a howl that shredded the morning quiet and sent a flock of swallows screeching from the barn loft's gaping doors.

Behind him strode Dawg, pushing Charity along ahead of him. His ear and cheek were covered with a thick bloodstained bandage. A savage grin slashed his face. "I wanted the blonde," he said, "but you'll do. Tonight, I'm gonna make you pay in bed for what your sister did to my ear."

"I'll kill myself first," Charity muttered, her stony face staring straight ahead.

"Get in here!" barked the old man, standing in the barn's open door, staring out at his slow-moving progeny. "I wanna get to Carlysle before noon, so the sheriff can still telegraph our claim today!"

When they'd all filed into the barn, including a sullen Burt, who'd drawn the long straw, the old man ordered Dawg to tie both women to stanchion posts while he, Burt, and Roy Luther cleared the wagon of everything but the coffin.

"No need for any of that frilly crap," the oldster

remarked when one of the steamer trunks burst open as it plunged to the barn's hard-packed earthen floor. "There's no fandango or dress-up-silly socializin' in these parts. No, sir, nothin' but good, hard work."

"And child rearin'," reminded Roy Luther, tossing a gunnysack over the wagon's far side. "Can't forget child rearin', Pa."

"That's true, son. These girls ain't just for you boys to dip your wicks in. I want me some grand—" The old man froze, crouched behind the wagon seat. "What was that?"

"What was what?" Burt stood glumly at the end of the wagon, watching his big brother and his father. There wasn't room for more than two in the wagon box without getting in each other's way.

Two low knocks sounded from the shadows.

"That," the old man said. He looked at Dawg, scuffling around the posts to which he was still tying the girls. "Shut up!"

Dawg stopped and, hunkered on his haunches, looked up, frowning.

Another soft knock. It sounded like a mouse scratching around the wagon.

The old man, Roy Luther, and Burt looked around the wagon, turning their heads this way and that.

Two thumps. Another. Loud as someone knocking on a door.

"Jumpin' Jesus," whispered Burt.

Dawg stood and walked to the side of the wagon. "It's comin' from inside the coffin."

Wide-eyed, the old man glanced at Roy Luther. Roy Luther returned the look, then gazed down at the coffin. He had a hand on his pistol butt.

"Open it," the old man said.

"I ain't gonna open that thing."

"Open it," the old man ordered.

Roy Luther cursed, licked his lips, and took mincing steps toward the coffin. He crouched down, wincing, and placed his hands along both sides of the lid. Slowly, tongue protruding from between his lips, he began lifting the lid.

He'd gotten it halfway off, peering warily down into the dark rectangle, when a hatted man with black whiskers and an anvil jaw suddenly rose up, a long-barreled .44 crossed over his chest. Extending the revolver, the man knocked the coffin lid from Roy Luther's hands, aimed the pistol at Roy Luther—who'd only just opened his mouth to scream—and fired.

The gun's roar filled the cavernous barn.

The girls screamed in unison.

"Ah, God!" cried the old man, staggering back from the coffin and clutching his stiff left arm. "Ah, God!"

The pistol turned toward him, then slid away toward Burt, still standing, hang-jawed, at the end gate. When the gun roared, Burt flew straight back out through the barn's open doors and fell in the yard with a thud.

Two more quick shots—*kaboom! kaboom!*—and Dawg dove sideways, cursing, his own pistol halfway out of its holster.

Dawg hit the floor, rolled, and turned his gaze back to the wagon. A man sat up in the coffin, calmly extending the .44 toward Dawg.

"You bastard!" Dawg shouted, raising his pistol toward the wagon.

Skye Fargo's pistol roared again, blowing a quarter-sized hole through Dawg's heart, slamming the young man's head back against the floor with an audible crunch of breaking bone.

The Trailsman turned his gun back to the old man, who was down on his knees, face drawn, eyes glazed with insane terror, forked veins bulging in his crimson forehead. He turned away from the coffin, clutching his stiff left arm. "No, Pete, please! You got it wrong. We was takin' your girls to town. We was . . . gonna set 'em *loose*." He rose up suddenly, and threw him-

57

self over the side of the wagon, hitting the ground with a loud grunt and a thud.

A moment later, the Trailsman watched the gray-bearded gent crawl out beyond the wagon toward the open barn doors, wheezing, red faced, and pressing his right hand to his chest.

He stopped and turned his crimson face back to the wagon. "Please, Pete, you gotta believe me. I don't blame you fer comin' back to look after your girls . . . but this was my boys' idea!" He sobbed. "Have mercy on me, Pete!"

His body convulsed. He gagged and choked, his face pinching. "Have . . . mercy . . ."

His head fell back in the dirt and he lay staring wide-eyed up at the ceiling.

The Trailsman depressed his Colt's hammer. He lifted one leg out of the coffin, then the other. He rose and peered over the side of the wagon, at the two young women staring up at him from the post they were tied to, back-to-back. They sat on their butts, knees raised, their jaws hanging slack.

"Girls, girls, girls." The Trailsman shook his head. Wincing, he adjusted the white bandage showing beneath his hat brim. "You two are one headache after another."

Fargo holstered his revolver, kicked Roy Luther off the side of the wagon box, and eased himself to the ground.

"Skye!" Harmony cried. "It's you!"

"Who's it look like?"

"How did you ever find us?"

"You gals carve a wide swath." Fargo drew his Arkansas toothpick from a boot well, squatted down between the two girls, and hacked at the ropes Dawg had tied around their wrists and the square-hewn ceiling joist. The toothpick slid through the rope like a hot blade through butter, releasing the rope from the post.

"Where's our father?" Charity asked, flinging the rope from her wrists.

"Hang on," Fargo said. "I'll get him."

He slipped the knife back in his boot, then climbed a wall ladder through a square ceiling hole, the plank rungs complaining under his weight. The girls stood dazed, watching the ceiling, which groaned and sighed as the Trailsman clomped around upstairs, dust and hay flecks sifting through the cracks. There was a heavy grating sound, as if something heavy were being dragged across the floor, and then a long, slender object suddenly dropped through the chute through which Fargo had disappeared.

Charity gasped.

Harmony said, "Oh, Lord!"

Before them, in the mound of hay beneath the chute, lay their father, faceup, one hand curled over his belly, the other over his left hip. He wasn't wearing his hat, and his long wavy hair was flecked with dust and straw.

The man's tall gray hat dropped through the chute. It fell across the dead man's pale face.

"Good heavens, Mr. Fargo," Charity yelled at the ceiling. "Have you no respect for the dead?"

Fargo climbed gingerly down the rungs, turned to the girls, and brushed straw from his buckskins. "My head hurt so bad from the brainin' the big bastard gave me that I felt I needed the element of surprise."

Charity was livid. "Surprise, indeed!"

"Yeah, I'd say I surprised 'em." Fargo bent down, snaked his arms beneath the body, and carried it over to the wagon. He set the body inside, then climbed into the box, picked Three-Gun up once more, and laid him in his casket. Harmony retrieved her father's hat and handed it up to Fargo, who set the hat on Three-Gun's head. He replaced the coffin lid and jumped back down to the floor.

Harmony beamed up at him. "I'm so glad you're

all right. I just knew you'd find a way to save us from these vermin. I just knew you would."

"Best get your possibles back in the wagon." Fargo grunted as he turned and headed for the open barn doors. "I'm gonna have me a smoke and fetch my horse."

Harmony and Charity shared a conspiratorial glance. Charity followed Fargo to the open doorway, beyond which he stood regarding the morning, digging rolling papers from his makings sack.

"Does that mean you're going to guide us, after all?" the brunette asked, tentative.

Fargo kept his back to the barn, his head bowed as he rolled the quirley. His shoulders jerked with a silent chuff. "You two'd get yourselves killed if I didn't."

He lit the quirley and walked out behind the barn to fetch the Ovaro. These women were going to be the death of him. But how did you send two beauties like that—woodenheaded and mooncalf foolish as they were—to the proverbial wolves?

He took a deep drag off the cigarette, the burn in his lungs soothing the ache in his head, which a traveling snake-oil salesman had been good enough to bandage—when Fargo had agreed to buy a bottle of the man's own patented elixir, that was.

"The Lord puts faith on fools, even those who help crazy, good-lookin' women," he reminded himself as he climbed on the pinto's back. He gigged the horse back toward the barn. "As long as they don't stay at it too long."

8

In the Prospector Saloon and Restaurant in Jackpot, three tall, well-armed men in matching flat-brimmed black hats sat around a table, variously occupied.

One was rolling a cigarette. Another was cleaning his silver-plated .44. The third was sharpening a giant, polished bowie knife on a whetstone, spitting on the stone regularly, and testing the blade by shaving the curly black hair on his left forearm.

They were big, heavy-shouldered men with full beards and mustaches. They looked so much alike, they might have been related, but they weren't. They were, however, part of the same gang led by the "Reverend" Justin Lawrence Peabody III.

The "Reverend" was not a man of the cloth. His father had been a Lutheran minister in a small village in Minnesota . . . before Justin Lawrence had killed him, that was, and thrown his mutilated body on the tin roof of their hut to season in the sun.

That was when Justin Lawrence acquired the handle.

The Reverend wasn't currently in the saloon, however. The fourth man in the saloon's group lounged on a small couch in the shadows at the back of the room. His black whipcord trousers were bunched around his boots. His black hat hung on the hat tree to the right of the couch and under an oil painting of a naked Indian princess riding a white horse.

A small blond whore knelt before the couch. She wore only a short burlap skirt. Her bare feet were curled beneath her, and her slender naked back faced the room. She moved her head up and down over the fourth man's naked crotch, making sucking sounds, stopping to coo and sigh and work him with her hands.

The man on the couch, Billy Bailey, a regulator from Oklahoma, squeezed his eyes closed, flinching as though someone were pricking him with small, sharp needles. "Damn, you ain't bad," he'd grunt every few minutes. "Damn . . ."

At the table, Reynolds Archer lit his quirley, glanced toward the back of the room, and said to the other two men at the table, "You'd swear he'd never had a French lesson before."

"Bailey's from Oklahoma," said James Price as he spit on his whetstone and rubbed it around with his thumb. "Just a shy cracker hick from the sticks, too embarrassed to ask for it 'less he's desperate. I told him, you know, it ain't like you're askin' your ma fer one."

Their laughter was interrupted by the opening and closing of the front door. They all turned to watch a tall man in a black, flat-brimmed hat like all of theirs walk to the bar and order a whiskey and a beer.

While the barman set a glass on the bar top and turned a bottle over it, filling it, the man stared across the room at the three men at the table. He heard Billy Bailey moaning and groaning, and glanced toward the back of the room, his gray-blue eyes glittering in the vagrant light from the front windows, then smiled and shook his head.

When he'd flipped several coins onto the bar, he took a long sip of the beer, licked the foam off his mustache, and, holding the half-drained beer in one hand, the full shot glass in the other, strode across the room to the table. He set his drinks down and plopped down in the empty chair.

He removed his hat, set it on the table, ran a thick hand through his wavy, salt-and-pepper hair. He had a bemused look on his face.

"We in the right town, Reverend?" Price asked, leaning over the table, his big knife in one hand, the whetstone in the other.

"We nailed it," said the gang leader, Reverend Peabody, throwing back his entire shot. "Found a saloon keeper who said they were through here just yesterday, headin' south."

"Well, what the hell we waitin' for?" snarled Archer, blowing cigarette smoke through his nostrils.

"Just one thing," said the Reverend, laying one hand on the table and giving the others a bemused expression.

"What's that?"

"They were with the Trailsman."

The others thought about that, and laughed.

"Them girls must be pretty," said Price, sheathing his knife.

"Come on," said Archer, draining his beer glass and stubbing out his quirley. "Let's cut their trail."

The Reverend leaned forward and jerked a thumb toward Bailey. "What about him? We wanna rush him?"

"Ah, shit," growled Price, jutting his chin toward the back of the room. "Come on, Billy, we got us a trail to fog!"

"Hold on, hold on!" Bailey yelled, his chin tipped back and his eyes squeezed shut, the girl's head moving up and down like a steam engine piston.

While the others stood and made for the door, boots pounding, spurs ringing, the Reverend calmly drained his beer. He set the empty mug on the table, then gave it a spin. Adjusting his string tie and jerking his brocade vest down at his waist, he glanced at Bailey and chuckled. "Come on, Billy. If that whore ain't brought you off yet, she ain't goin' to."

He strode to the door.

"Wait!" Bailey said, pushing up on his elbows and knocking the whore away with his knees. "Wait for me, goddamn it!"

The girl squealed when he accidentally kicked her with his boot. He set both feet on the floor, stood, and reached down to pull his pants up. He tripped, dropped to a knee, then turned over onto his butt and, grunting and cursing, pulled his pants up to his thighs.

He rose up on his elbows, lifted his butt off the floor, kicked his legs out, and pulled his pants and longhandles up to his waist.

Quickly, he buttoned his fly and buckled his black leather belt. He sprang to his feet and grabbed his hat from the rack. "Wait for me, goddamn you, sons o' bitches!"

Scooping his gun belt off a chair back, he ran toward the front door, tripping over tables and chairs.

Behind him, the whore sat up and turned to him, her hair hanging in her eyes. With the back of her hand, she wiped blood from her lower lip, and yelled, "Hope ye never come off again, ye uncouth bastard!"

Riding along in the fillies' wagon, the reins in his hands, Fargo looked over his right shoulder.

The girls hadn't gotten much sleep last night, tied as they were, both literally and metaphorically, to the ranchers' cookstove. They were getting some shut-eye now, under Charity's parasol in the wagon box, colorful quilts piled beneath them to protect their delicate skin from chafes and splinters.

Both girls lay flat on their backs. The morning heat had dampened their blouses, which clung to their breasts. Even for the priggish Charity, it was too hot for a corset. The brunette's full, deep orbs jiggled under the sweaty cloth like raccoons trying to fight their way out of a croaker sack.

As Fargo watched, the wagon's bounce and sway worked one of Charity's buttons loose, revealing the long, high, ivory slope of her left breast. At the crest of the breast, the soft nipple rubbed against the wet cloth, behind which clearly shone the red-brown areola, large as a 'dobe dollar.

The brunette's eyes opened suddenly, as if she'd suddenly become aware of his stare. She followed his glance to her breasts, frowned, lifted her head from the quilts, and began closing buttons. Fargo gave a chuff—what good's a woman if she can't be admired?—and turned around to face the plodding mule, squinting against the sunlight.

A minute later, Charity crawled into the driver's box. She smoothed her skirt beneath her legs and sat down beside Fargo. Her hair had come loose during her nap, and she reached up to secure it to the top of her head.

"Sorry you caught me starin'," Fargo said.

"You're sorry you were staring, or you're sorry you got caught?"

"The last one."

"You're incorrigible, Mr. Fargo."

"I'm alone a lot, you see."

"Still, it's improper to ogle women. Were you raised by wolves?"

"Pretty much."

"You've an answer for everything, don't you?"

"Mmm-hmm."

She glanced at him sitting there, leaning forward, his elbows on his knees, his buckskin sleeves rolled up his corded forearms. He stared straight out over the mule's back, his eyes constantly moving, darting to every rock and boulder, every sage clump and cottonwood hollow—anywhere a man or men might be lurking.

Charity cleared her throat and tugged the cloth of her blouse away from her breasts, sitting straight-backed in her seat. "Mr. Fargo, may I have a serious word with you?"

"Depends on the subject."

"The subject is my sister. I think she's come to set store by you. And, while I'm grateful that you've decided to guide us and our father to Del Norte, I would like to make one thing clear. My sister is strictly off-limits to your animal passions."

Fargo looked at her. "What about yourself? You strictly off-limits to my animal passions?"

Charity blinked slowly. "Don't flatter yourself."

"Does that mean you will or you won't share my bedroll tonight?"

Again, she blinked slowly, a flush rising in her cheeks as she stared hard across the mule's head. "It means, of course, that I won't be doing any such thing—tonight or *any* night. Ours, Mr. Fargo, is purely and simply a business arrangement."

Fargo hooked a smile at her. "You tryin' to tell me you haven't thought about it?"

She glanced at him, appalled, slapping a hand to her chest. "I certainly have not!"

Fargo dropped the reins on the floor of the driver's box, turned to her, and took her in his arms. Her head fell back. She gasped and opened her mouth to cry out, but before she could utter a word, he clamped his mouth down on hers.

Her body tensed, and she kicked her right leg out. She grabbed his shirt in her fists, trying to push him away from her, but her grip died in seconds, and her hands slowly flattened out against his shoulders. As her body began to melt in his arms, he pulled away.

He grinned. "You, ma'am, are a liar." He turned

toward the Ovaro trailing the wagon with its reins looped around the saddle horn, and whistled. As the horse trotted up alongside the wagon, Fargo turned back to Charity, who looked as though she'd just been slapped and wasn't sure what to do about it.

"When you're ready to stop thinkin' and start doin'," Fargo said, "let me know."

He set the wagon's reins in her limp hands, then turned and stepped onto the pinto, the saddle squeaking beneath his weight.

"Where are you going?" she said crisply, her lips pinched tight.

"Scout ahead."

He put the steel to the stallion, and, sliding his rifle from its boot with one hand, galloped off across a low hill. Charity stared through his sifting dust.

"Animal." She flicked the reins. Annoyed by the needling burn deep in her belly, she straightened her back, stuck her chest out, chin up, and shook the hair from her eyes. "An absolute brute."

She rode with her face set in an angry frown for a time. Gradually her expression softened. Unconsciously, she stuck the tip of her tongue out and ran it slowly across her lips, still able to taste the sagey, smoky flavor of him. . . .

He was gone for forty-five minutes. Seeing no sign of trouble, he rode back to the wagon and drove until sundown, Charity giving him the cold shoulder, then turned the wagon into a shallow ravine to camp.

He'd finished picketing the pinto and the mule in the tall bluestem lining a creek bank, when he turned toward the fir copse in which the girls had pitched their tent.

Harmony strode toward him around a mossy rock, sashaying from side to side, barefoot as usual, her hair down, her thin cotton skirt buffeting about her coltish legs. She held her lips together, spread wide, eyes flashing. She didn't stop, but came right up to him, threw her arms around his neck, and sprang off her toes. He caught her thighs as she wrapped her legs around his back and kissed him.

"That's for saving us," Harmony said.

"What choice did I have?" Fargo grunted, his manhood instantly responding to the girl's crotch pressed against his belly, her firm, round butt beneath his hands. The cotton was sheer from many washings, so it wasn't hard to tell she'd donned no underwear.

"I couldn't thank you properly before now." She cast a furtive glance over her shoulder. "I think Charity suspicions I've got a bad case of the swoons for you. We might have to be discreet for a time. When Charity suspicions I'm up to somethin' she don't think is 'upstanding and befitting a young lady's character,' she watches me like a hawk. She's washing down at the creek right now, though, so we got time for one more."

Harmony mashed her mouth against his, groaning, licking at him, nibbling his lower lip as she pulled away, and let her feet drop. Grinning, she glanced at the growing bulge in his buckskins.

"I might could slip out later this evenin', however."

"Better not," Fargo said. "Like you said, your sister'll be watching you like a hawk. And me," he added for his own amusement.

"Tomorrow night, then?"

"I make no promises."

Still grinning, showing her white teeth, she turned away and sashayed back through the trees. She turned a cunning look over her shoulder, nibbling her lower lip. "See you then." She giggled and skipped back toward the tent, the dress bounding dangerously high on her thighs.

Fargo cursed. Instead of building a fire right away, he decided to go splash some cold water on his face.

Still exhausted from their ordeal with the ranchers, Charity and Harmony turned in early, leaving the

Trailsman to sit around the fire, sipping coffee and cleaning his guns, alone.

As tired as she was, Charity couldn't sleep, however. Her mind was restless, with disparate images flying through it like hunting crows. The ranchers, her father's body dropped through the hay chute like so much refuse, her sister smiling up at the Trailsman as though he'd been sent from heaven itself.

Silly girl. *Disgusting* man!

Then, suddenly, he'd had her, Charity, in his arms and was pressing his lips down on hers while his muscular thigh crowded her uncomfortably.

And just as she'd begun—what . . . ? Enjoying it?— he'd pulled away. . . .

No, that wasn't it. She'd just been so frightened by the uncouth ranchers that she'd merely enjoyed a protective moment in the Trailsman's arms. That was all.

A sense of security and comfort after such a terrifying ordeal. Any man would have evoked a similar sentiment.

Relieved, the images dying, she exhaled slowly and closed her eyes. She didn't know how long she'd slept before she lifted her head suddenly and stared at the tent's buttoned fly, beyond which the fire was a jostling umber blur.

The sound rose again, louder this time. It sounded like water being poured onto the ground.

A man sighed deeply, gave a grunt.

Charity gave a quiet, disapproving huff.

The Trailsman . . . tending nature . . .

The brunette lay back against her pillow, frowning, confused again by that needling warmth in the pit of her stomach. She closed her eyes, exhaled slowly once more, and relaxed her limbs.

Sleep did not come.

With a sharp sigh, she sat up, donned her heavy flannel wrapper and bedroom slippers, and, leaving her long hair hanging loose, unbuttoned the tent's fly and crawled outside. When she'd rebuttoned the fly, she stood and turned to where Fargo lay against his saddle, long legs stretched before him, boots crossed. The brim of his hat was pulled down over his eyes.

"Can't sleep?"

She crossed to the fire and sank down to her knees, ten feet to his right, hands on her thighs. "I must've gotten overly tired. Or those men have thoroughly frayed my nerves." She glanced at him with furrowed brows, and added irritably, "I was doing all right, though, until you . . . did what you did over there."

"Sorry," Fargo said, his eyes still closed beneath his hat brim. "I figured you two would be out like blown lamps."

"Perhaps next time you could tend to nature a little farther from the tent."

"I'll be sure and do that." Fargo's lips stretched. "Hope it didn't make you think thoughts not befitting the good character of a young lady such as yourself."

"Don't be ridiculous. If I did think such thoughts, it certainly wouldn't be about such a lusty, unwashed frontiersman as yourself."

"Who would you have such thoughts about—if'n, of course, you were given to such lowly musings?"

"*Civilized* men, of cour—"

She stopped when Fargo sat up suddenly, thumbing his hat up his forehead and staring sharply into the darkness. He'd reached for the Henry propped beside him, but stopped his hand on the rear stock, listening.

"What is it?" Charity whispered, looking around warily, holding her robe close about her heaving breasts.

Fargo was silent for a moment. He relaxed, removing his hand from the Henry. "Wolf on the night stump. Nothin' to fear."

"I didn't hear anything."

Fargo reached forward and tossed another log on the fire, the sparks careening skyward like red ants drifting toward the overarching pine boughs and, beyond, the stars.

"What did you hear?"

"Heard it step down on a twig."

"How did you know it was a wolf?"

"By the pitch of the sound. Too soft for a coyote or a fox. Way too soft for a bear, even a black bear. Just right for a mountain lion or a wolf."

"How do you know it wasn't a mountain lion?" Challenge sounded in her voice, sparked faintly in her mocking eyes.

"A mountain lion wouldn't have been so careless with folks about. The wolf must have fed and been headin' back to his den, or she wouldn't have, either."

"You even know it was a 'she.'"

Fargo heaved himself up with a grunt and reached for the rifle. "Too light. A male wolf wouldn't make a sound of that pitch." He turned and began strolling off toward the horse and the mule cropping grass quietly in the darkness. "Best go back to bed. It's cool and gonna be gettin' cooler. Fall's comin' on."

"Where are you going?" she said too sharply.

Fargo turned back to her. "On the scout. Make sure we're alone. Why?" A calculating grin slitted his eyes. "Got somethin' else in mind?"

She frowned and drew the night robe taut about her breasts. "Don't flatter yourself."

"In that case"—he pinched his hat brim and drifted into the shadows, his boots barely making a sound— "good night."

9

Skye Fargo had to admit, albeit reluctantly, that sleep did not come easily when two such heart-achingly beautiful fillies lay curled in their blankets only a few feet away from his own bedroll. The fierce heart of his Trailsman's passion beat like a tom-tom, and his blood flowed hot in his veins.

He tossed and turned through the first part of the night, getting up often to walk around, watch, and listen—to try *not* to remember the sensation of Harmony lying on her back in the cool ferns beneath him, writhing impaled on the end of his manhood.

To try *not* to imagine Charity, with her rich hair tumbling around her conical breasts, in the same position, thighs grasping his ribs as if to ride him skyward to the stars.

Up again around four o'clock, two heavy blankets draped around his broad naked shoulders, he rolled a quirley. His breath puffed in the chill mountain air that smelled faintly of snow. The cold was good, though. It would keep old Three-Gun from getting overly ripe before Fargo and the ladies from Heart's

Desire made Del Norte, on the southern slopes of the Sangre de Cristos.

Fargo reached into the fire's glowing ashes for a stick. With the stick's smoldering end, he set fire to the quirley and blew smoke at the stars, so clear as to resemble Christmas candles trimming the pine boughs. Fargo glanced at the tent, where the two beauties lay beyond the buttoned fly, sensuously curled in sleep.

He chuffed at the old, masculine pull, and yearned for a long, quiet winter in New Mexico, with only occasional trips to Taos for supplies and to gas over strong ale with the arthritic, old fur trappers in the Spanish Trail Saloon. Nothing like a female for tensing up a man, throwing a stout branch through the wheel spokes of simple living . . . to make you sweat when it wasn't even hot.

He smoked the quirley down to a nub, tossed it into the near-dead fire, took a long listen to the night, then rolled up in his soogan.

He was up well before dawn, bathing naked in the creek's chill waters that smelled of wood rot and mushrooms. When he'd dried off and dressed, he gave the tent a kick to wake the girls, then threw a fistful of coffee beans, which he'd mashed with his pistol butt, into the bubbling coffeepot.

He and the girls washed corn cakes and salt pork down with the coffee, then loaded up the wagon. Fargo had saddled the Ovaro and hitched up the mule, then, realizing his canteen was empty, headed toward the creek.

He stopped when he saw Harmony crouched along the water, her naked back to him, her blouse and chemise draped over a chokecherry shrub. She'd pinned her blond hair up, but several strands curled down around her neck and ears. She was cupping water to her face and breasts, lifting her face to the rising sun.

Fargo moved forward, his boots crunching grass. Harmony turned with a start, eyes wide, elbows automatically crossing over her breasts. Seeing him, she let her expression relax. She smiled.

"Reckon I'm still jumpy. I should know you'd never let any strangers into the camp."

Fargo grunted and kept his direct gaze from the girl, even when she lowered her arms from her breasts. They were heading into the heart of the Ute country controlled by the old war chief Burnt-Bear, and he had to keep his mind sharp. He knelt beside the stream and submerged the water flask, the water gurgling through the spout.

Harmony knelt a few feet to his right, splashed another handful of water in her face, brushed her fingers across her breasts. "I heard you and Charity up last night, talkin' around the fire."

Fargo grunted again.

Harmony said with forced nonchalance, "What were you two chattin' about?"

Fargo gave her a skeptical glance.

"She wasn't tryin' to . . . you know . . . flirt with you or nothin', was she?"

Fargo corked the canteen. "Best mount up. We're burnin' good light."

He straightened and started back toward the camp. Beyond the trees, on the other side of the doused fire, Charity was doing some last-minute arranging of the camping supplies in the wagon box. Harmony ran up beside Fargo, gave his arm a tug, and said, "She *was*, wasn't she?"

"Get in the wagon."

"Skye, you wouldn't corrupt her, would you? I mean, Charity ain't like me. I damn near gave every boy in Heart's Desire a poke, but sis . . . she's *pure* and *innocent*!"

Fargo stopped and grunted impatiently. "Your sis has made it very plain that I disgust her no end. Her biggest worry is that *I'm* gonna corrupt *you*." Fargo chuckled, took the blonde's arm, and jerked her toward the wagon. "Now why don't you join your sis on the hearse, and arrange your parasol?"

Wrinkling her nose at Fargo, Harmony started toward the wagon. When Charity had turned her back to make sure their father's coffin lid was tight, Harmony turned back suddenly, smiled up at the Trailsman, and gave his cheek a quick peck. She skipped ahead, her blond curls falling from their bun, and scrambled into the driver's box.

Behind her, Fargo sighed.

The wagon was rocking along an old Spanish trail in the cedar-stippled foothills of the Sangre de Cristos when Charity turned to the Trailsman. "How much farther do you think, Mr. Fargo?"

She sat on the driver's seat between Fargo on the wagon's left side, and Harmony on the right. When they'd started out, she'd been riding on the outside, but when Harmony had returned from a recent nature walk, the brunette, instead of letting Harmony climb over her feet, had slid over to rest her thigh against Fargo's. Fargo had noticed the maneuver with a wry quirk of his brow. Harmony had noticed it, too, and given Fargo a sharp, admonishing glance.

Now, rolling a lucifer between his lips, Fargo answered the brunette's question. "Three full days, maybe part of a fourth."

"I do hope Papa's remains keep," said the blonde.

"Harmony!" chastised her sister.

"It's only natural, sis. I mean, it's cool enough at night, but if it keeps gettin' this hot during the day, he's gonna swell up like a—"

"Quiet!" Fargo hissed, drawing back on the mule's reins.

"What?"

"Stow it!"

"What's wrong?"

"I'm what's wrong," Fargo announced, staring at a sun-blasted rimrock towering on his left. "I've ridden uptrail and down twice this morning, and I missed their sign."

"Whose sign?" Charity said, following his gaze up the steep, boulder-strewn incline, shading her eyes with her hand. "I don't see anything."

Fargo didn't say anything. He continued staring at the pine-studded crest of the rimrock. Finally, he cursed and flicked the reins over the mule's back, and the wagon began clattering forward once more. He stared grimly into the hazy distance, brooding, eyes rolling from side to side.

"What is it, Skye?" Harmony asked, keeping her voice low.

"Injuns."

"Oh, no," Charity said.

"We're in Burnt-Bear's country. We should be all right, though . . . long as the chief's still got his braves on a short leash." A thought dawned on him, and he cursed again before he could catch himself.

"What is it?" Harmony and Charity asked in unison.

Fargo winced, castigating himself for his loose tongue. No point in riling the girls.

"Just remembered ol' Burnt-Bear took sick two winters ago. Had a big lump on his side, big as a turnip." Fargo cast another wary glance at the ridgetop, and slowly shook his head. "Sure hope the old bastard didn't kick off."

"Why don't we turn around, take a different route?" Harmony asked, her eyes nervously scanning the rimrock.

"They've seen us. From the number of shadows I saw, there's too many to fight, and we can't outrun 'em in the wagon."

The wagon bounced over a hole in the faint trail,

jouncing the passengers and freight, the coffin slamming against the box. The girls gave a cry, as if the Indians had caused the jolt.

"What're we gonna do?" Charity's voice was thin.

"Sit tight. Relax," Fargo said. "Enjoy the ride."

They continued for fifteen more minutes until, cresting a low hill and starting down the other side, Fargo spied movement fifty yards ahead and left.

Horseback riders filed out from the side of a low scarp at the south edge of the rimrock, angling down the hill toward the trail. When the last rider had appeared from behind the scarp, trotting his horse to catch up to the others, Fargo counted nine braves.

Red-bronze skin glistening with oil, and eagle feathers decorating their shoulder-length hair, they were all armed with spears, bows, and knives. Arrow-packed deer-hide quivers hung down their naked backs. The arrows clicked together as the horses descended the hill, swerving around piñons and juniper shrubs, the unshod hooves clomping dully.

While the lead rider's face was pitted and heavy browed, his eyes creased with savage intensity, none of the riders looked a day over eighteen.

As the short-legged mustangs angled toward the wagon, the leader stiffened on his quilted leather saddle blanket decorated in multicolored bead designs. A necklace of wolf teeth jostled about his scrawny neck.

Glaring at Fargo, the brave fingered the horn-handled knife secured to his right thigh with a brushy red foxtail. The spear of the potbellied buck riding behind him was decorated with tribal feathers. They were from Burnt-Bear's band, all right. None were far from the teat, but brash cunning and subtle mockery glinted in the dark eyes sweeping Fargo and the two girls sitting to his right.

Fargo fought back his impulse to reach for the .44 in his holster. The group had the look of a game-hunting band, as they weren't painted for war. But a flick of Fargo's thumb toward his Colt might set off a powder keg of youthful machismo.

The rider cut his glare from the girls to Fargo as he reined his horse to Fargo's right. As the others spread out to both sides of him, the contentious young buck leaned forward over his knife sheath and cut loose a stream of enraged Ute, sprinkled liberally with English epithets.

Harmony and Charity sank back against the seat, terrified.

Fargo sat slump-shouldered, chin down, a bored, faintly sneering expression on his sun-seared, unshaven face. Fargo didn't take his direct gaze from the spit-spewing leader, but at the periphery of his vision he saw the other braves grinning, amused at the tongue-lashing their leader was giving this White-Eyes and his two scrawny whores who dared venture into their hunting grounds.

When the buck had finished his tirade, Charity and Harmony stared, aghast, as Fargo gave back as good as he'd been given in the brave's own tongue. Half standing and waving his arms, his face flushed and creased with fury, the Trailsman loosed a long volley of hard consonants and variously pitched grunts and sighs, until he sank back down to his seat, falling silent but keeping his jutted jaw hard, his chin deeply dimpled, waiting.

The leader's eyes flickered apprehensively as he sank back on his leather saddle pad. As the braves around him broke the heavy silence with chuckles, turning jeering glances at him, an embarrassed flush turned the leader's hard face the brick red of old tack. Keeping his face directed at Fargo, he cut his eyes to the other braves.

His chest rose and fell sharply. His gaze settled on the Trailsman's, his eyes boring deep into Fargo's.

The brave's lip curled suddenly. In a blur of motion, his right hand grabbed the dagger from his thigh sheath. Screaming what Fargo roughly translated as "Die, dog-fucking hell spawn!" he bolted over his horse's shoulder toward Fargo, the dagger blade aimed at the Trailsman's head.

When the dagger was six inches from the brim of Fargo's hat, he grabbed the brave's wrist with his left hand, breaking the bones like brittle twigs and jerking his Arkansas toothpick, which he'd concealed beneath his right thigh, straight up.

The curved tip pierced the brave's lower belly, driving to the hilt. Hot, thick blood washed over the Trailsman's fist. The brave's shriek grew to a deafening pitch as Fargo, gripping the brave's limp wrist in one hand, drove the knife blade up with the other, till it knocked against the breastbone.

The young Ute's entrails spilled over the wagon seat and wheel before Fargo removed the blade in a final blood shower. He let the body drop. It bounced off the wagon's front wheel with a dull thud and hit the ground with a wet smack.

Silence.

The other braves stared down at him, wide-eyed, their glances flicking to their dead leader lying like a gut pile at the base of the wagon wheel.

Several of the horses whinnied and snorted, restless and frightened. The braves held them in check, drawing arrows back with sinewy crackling sounds, and raising strap-iron spearheads.

"Oh, Skye," Harmony cried softly, cowering. "I don't think you should've done that!"

10

The Trailsman drew back his right wrist, preparing to throw the toothpick. He'd gut the potbellied brave, then reach for his .44 and take down as many of the fledgling warriors as possible before they turned him and the girls into human pincushions.

But as one of the braves raised his spear above his shoulder, the potbellied kid, having seen the toothpick poised for a killing launch, slapped the raised spear with one hand. He threw his other hand straight out toward the other braves and made a slashing motion.

"No!" he shouted in Ute.

The others looked at him skeptically.

His fearful gaze met Fargo's. His eyes flickered, regaining a bold light as he thrust his chest out and lowered a look at the dead brave at the base of the wagon wheel.

"Kill a man who has done us a favor?" He dropped his eyes to their dead leader and wrinkled his nose. "For killing that gutless faker, Circling Hawk, we should each give him our fattest sister for a night, let him know the pleasure of sleeping with *real* women."

Fargo glanced at the girls, still staring terrified at the braves, having no clue they'd just been insulted.

As the other braves shared conspiratorial glances then finally grumbled their agreement, most looking relieved, the potbellied brave looked at Fargo. "You and your scrawny whores may continue your journey, White-Eyes called Trailsman, friend of Chief Burnt-Bear who has passed. We regret that we delayed your journey."

He spit on the bloody heap of their dead leader, and turned his mount. The others followed him back the way they'd come, several casting furtive glances behind them, the last two conversing heatedly and gesturing.

"Boy, that was close!" Harmony said, heaving a long sigh.

Charity glanced down at the dead buck, then shifted her gaze to Fargo. "What did you say to them, anyway, that made them back down?"

Fargo stared after the retreating hunters, his lake blue eyes slitted apprehensively. "Just reminded 'em I saved old Burnt-Bear's life once, durin' a buffalo stampede not far from here, and that he was three times the man they'd ever be. Might have pushed it a little, though, when I called 'em all pups with the hearts of pigtailed girls for stopping a wagon with two defenseless women aboard."

"That's what angered . . . him?" Charity asked, canting her head at the dead buck without looking at the body.

"Reckon." Fargo flicked the reins over the mule's back, and the wagon rolled forward. "We'd best put some ground behind us." He turned his gaze left, where the Indians' dust still sifted, burnt orange in the sunlight angling over the rimrock. "When they start brooding about what just happened, they're liable to decide to even the score . . . and regain their honor."

Staring straight ahead, Charity shook her head slowly. "Men."

"Well, we do it for the women."

"How do you explain that, Mr. Fargo?"

"Imagine what's gonna happen when those boys ride back to their band and have to tell the others—includin' the *girls*—that their leader got himself gutted while they just sat around and watched?" Fargo grimaced. "Those boys'll be lucky to get laid before they turn forty!"

"Yes, but those are savage women." Charity pouted. "With only one thing on their minds."

Fargo turned to her. "Miss Charity?"

"Yes?"

"You mind pulling your claws out of my leg now?"

Charity looked down. Her cheeks turned crimson. All five nails of her left hand were still buried in Fargo's thigh.

She pulled her hand away, as if from something hot, and pursed her lips as she muttered, "Sorry."

As the day wore on, Fargo pushed the wagon higher into the foothills of the Sangre de Cristos.

He was following an ancient Indian trail once used by Spanish traders before falling into disuse except by the occasional mountain man, the faint trace now overgrown with silver sage, stunt cedars, bear grass, and wildflowers, with sweet ferns and wild peas growing in the shade. Old fire rings still lined the trail, usually indicating good water and grazing. Also, there were sporadic, crudely marked graves of travelers who'd run afoul of Indians, beasts, illness, or accident.

On a previous trip, Fargo had found an ancient Spanish broadsword, too rusty and chipped to be worth much, but he'd traded it for a new saddle and ammo for his Henry.

Before him and to the right of the purple, pine-carpeted ramparts of the higher mountains lay low, rounded mesas that followed one another like ocean waves. Pedestal rocks and stone outcroppings rose in the distance, and Fargo frequently had to slow their pace to cross dry-bed creeks gouged by old placer mines.

Fargo was craning his neck to inspect the old timbers and wood scaffolding marking the entrance to an old silver mine dig, when he saw purple in the sky behind him. He turned full around to get a good luck. The northern sky looked like night was seeping down from the wrong direction. Even as he watched, the purple mass—touched with even deeper purple swirls and bone white mares' tails—grew larger.

A chill breeze touched his face.

He cursed and gigged up the mule, casting another glance over his shoulder to make sure the Ovaro was following along behind. The wagon's bounce and sway woke the girls napping in the box. They groaned. Harmony lifted her head above the back of the driver's seat, her pretty, heart-shaped face creased from the quilt she'd been resting on, blond curls hanging awry.

"What is it?"

"Storm comin' on."

Harmony turned a glance at the northern sky. "So let's pull into the trees and camp. We didn't stop for lunch, and I'm hungry."

"No time. Someone's behind us. We have to get to the top of that pass yonder, nest up in the slab rock."

Harmony's face paled. "Who's behind us?"

"I don't know, but I saw a sun reflection off a spyglass just after we left the Injuns. Must be white men."

Behind the wagon, thunder rumbled. The breeze picked up, bending the pine tops to the left of the trail.

"What's happening?" Charity asked sleepily. "Did I hear you say someone's behind us?"

They were heading through solid fir-and-pine forest now, and the trail had turned rocky and dark, the columns of straight-trunked evergreens blocking out the light. Fargo's gaze was fixed on the rocky pass looming three or four miles ahead.

"Don't get your panties all in a twist, sis," the Trailsman grumbled.

Harmony had climbed onto the seat beside Fargo. Now Charity climbed up beside Harmony, clutching the seat back so she didn't fall, and regarding the Trailsman disdainfully. "You're a charming man, Mr. Fargo."

"Charming ain't gonna get us to the top of that pass."

"Why don't we turn into the forest?" Charity said. "Surely, there are places to hide in the trees."

Fargo flicked the reins and yelled at the mule, slowing now as the grade steepened and the slippery rocks complicated the climb. "They'll track us."

"You could shoot them," Harmony said.

"There might be more than I could take." Fargo shook his head, his cheeks lined with annoyance. Damn women talked more than the wind blew on the high plains. "We're gonna make that high ground up ahead, wait out the storm from there. The rocks capping the pass are like a crow's nest."

The mule climbed. The wagon rocked along behind, bounding violently over upthrusts in the exposed limestone and granite. At every bounce Fargo gritted his teeth. If they threw a wheel or busted an axle pin . . .

They'd climbed the grade for fifteen minutes when a cold wind shunted against Fargo's back, drying the sweat on his buckskin tunic. A minute later, a few raindrops slanted down, pelting his hat. The girls grumbled and hunkered down on the seat.

Fargo glanced at them. "Better break out your rain slickers."

The girls looked at each other blankly. Holding her wind-whipped hair back from her face, Charity turned to Fargo. "We don't have rain slickers."

He snorted. "You each have three steamer trunks full of dress pretties but no rain slickers?"

Charity furled her brows. "I see no reason to take that tone with us. We are not *frontiersmen*!"

84

"You got that right." Fargo jerked his head toward the wagon box. "Better wrap yourselves in quilts. It's gonna turn right cold and wet mighty soon!"

As if to prove him right, lightning forked behind them, lighting up the entire sky. Charity gasped, startled, as she pulled several quilts up from the wagon box. Thunder clapped and rumbled. The plodding mule brayed and snorted but did not slow its pace. It seemed to know it had to make the high ground before stopping.

Fargo turned and snarled.

The clouds raced toward him like a lid slid over a casket, shepherding a slanted gray rain curtain, the wind ruffling the pine tops like an unseen giant hand moving toward the wagon. The brunt of the rain hit, instantly soaking the Trailsman and the girls, who cowered beneath their quilts. Behind the wagon, the Ovaro whinnied and pranced but continued to follow the wagon while sliding wary glances behind.

Lightning flashed and thunder rumbled like the angry voice of God. Rain sluiced off the Trailsman's hat and shone silver on the back of the mule, the large white drops bouncing like hail. The rocky trail instantly became a creek, brown water rushing over the rocks. The mule's shod hooves slipped and slid. The wagon fishtailed. The Trailsman rose up in his seat, lashing the reins against the beast's back and raging, "Get along, mule! Hi-yaaa!"

Maybe he should have taken the girls' advice and hidden the wagon below. Too late. If he tried to turn around now, the mule and wagon would likely roll back down the mountain.

The rain pummeled the wagon. It slashed down so hard and fast that the Trailsman could see little beyond the mule but a gray haze. He kept looking behind to see if the horseback riders were trying to run him down, but in this weather he wouldn't see them till they were on top of him.

Inwardly, he cursed, but was relieved when the downpour relented enough that he could see the rock slabs at the crest of the pass, thirty yards away and closing. The trail curved to the right, became soft red clay. As the mule followed the turn, clomping through the muddy water up to its hocks, a sudden blue-white flash filled Fargo's vision.

It was a vast fireball for a moment, searing Fargo's retinas and bathing his face in a stovelike heat.

A deafening *carr-rrunk*!

Then thunder clapped so close to the wagon that Fargo's ears rang. The concussion threw him back in his seat.

One of the girls screamed.

There was the smell of brimstone and the sound of burning and tearing, then a sizzling as the rain doused the fire.

Slitting his eyes against the brightness, Fargo peered to his right. Twenty feet from the trail, sparks flew from a tall fir, and a large branch, seared from the trunk as if by a giant whipsaw, turned a slow somersault halfway to the ground.

It landed with a cracking, hollow thud ten feet from the trail.

The mule bolted forward, braying, jerking the wagon from right to left, the wheels sliding and fishtailing, the girls shrieking as they and Fargo were nearly thrown from the seat.

"Ease up, mule!"

The wagon's right rear wheel slid off the trail and slammed into a gully. Both girls screamed as they were nearly thrown over the seat back, heads snapping over their shoulders. The braying mule lowered its head and tried to bull forward. The wagon wouldn't budge. The mule's hooves slipped out from beneath it. It fell with a splash.

Fargo didn't even try to goad it forward. He dropped the reins. "Gawd*damn*!"

He leaped over the left front wheel. His left boot landed first, then promptly slid out from beneath him. He fell on his ass, throwing his arms out to break the fall.

He cursed again, louder, and heaved himself to his feet. Boots splashing, the water rising to his shins, his buckskins plastered against his brawny frame so that nearly every muscle showed in relief, he ran around behind and inspected the right rear wheel.

He snapped another curse and turned to peer back down the hill. Along the trail, shadowy horseback figures drifted off into the trees.

He turned to the girls staring down at him looking waterlogged and miserable under their quilts. "Harmony, hand down my rifle and grab the reins!"

11

Rifle in hand, the Trailsman walked back to where the pinto stood, hanging its head in the middle of the trail, hock-deep in mud, rain splashing off its saddle.

Fargo grabbed his folding hatchet from the ring beneath the right saddlebag, cast another look down trail, then slogged through the mud to the fallen branch. When he'd hacked off several broad secondary branches, he ordered Charity to position them beneath the stuck wheel.

Without a fuss, the girl cast off her wet quilts and scrambled off the wagon. As Fargo began chopping at the primary branch, intending to cut it in two, the brunette retrieved the branches and, wincing against the rain and wind pummeling her and pasting her skirt and blouse flat against her curvaceous figure, positioned the branches beneath the wheel.

Fargo chopped at the stout main branch, pausing every third or fourth chop to peer downhill, where he'd seen the shadows. When he'd hacked it through, he stripped off the rest of the secondary branches, sharpened one end with three deft blows, and carried the five-foot length to the wheel, slipping the hatchet and rifle under the canvas.

Charity stood before him, fists on her hips, awaiting more orders, her breasts fully revealed beneath the soaking wet fabric of her blouse. If he didn't know better, he'd have said she was at least *half*-consciously showing them to him. Catching his glance, she beetled her brows.

Fargo told her to stand back.

As he levered the stout branch into the mud beneath the wheel, he ordered Harmony to nudge the mule forward.

Crouched, his feet spread, each boot propped against a stone, he pushed down on the branch, grinding the end into the mud, and rocking the wheel back and forth.

"Nudge him!" he barked.

"I am nudging him!" Harmony returned.

"Nudge him harder!" Fargo shouted, throwing his entire weight into the branch, gritting his teeth as the wood began cracking.

Harmony stood in the driver's box and whipped the reins against the demoralized mule's water-silvered back. "Go, you damn beast!"

Fargo cursed and rocked the wheel, watching it roll ever so slightly forward onto the green branches. Harmony yelled at the mule, whipping the reins against its back, the mule braying as if in protest. It was making progress, however, and when the wheel was entirely on the secondary branches, Fargo slipped the lever's sharpened end farther into the mud beneath it, and bellowed, "Puuullllll, you mangy *beast!*"

At the same time, he straightened and pulled up on the lever, the cords standing out in his swollen arms, lips drawn back from his teeth. "Puuuulllllllll!"

As the mule lowered its head and leaned into its collar, the wheel rose up slowly out of the water-filled hole, climbed the branches, and settled back on the trail, continuing to roll forward as the mule plunged onward up trail.

"Keep him movin'!" Fargo yelled to Harmony.

He tossed away the branch and threw his right hand out to Charity. "Climb aboard!"

Taking his hand with her left, the brunette threw her right one up and got purchase on the driver's seat. Running forward along the slippery trail, Fargo was about to sling her up like a bag of corn when she lost her grip and hit the trail with both feet. Turning, she fell forward into Fargo's arms. The jolt threw him slightly backward, and when he moved his feet to absorb the blow, both boots slipped out beneath him. He hit the trail on his back, Charity landing on his chest, her breasts pressing against him—two full, firm mounds.

Her nose was a half inch from his.

"This ain't the time nor the place, fool woman!"

"I wasn't—" She stopped, scowling down at him. "Ohhh!"

Fargo scrambled out from beneath her, pulled her to her feet, and half dragged her up to the wagon. At a level spot, he stopped, threw her aboard, then climbed in after her. A minute later, he was back in the driver's seat, reins in his hands, casting anxious glances behind.

No sign of the men who'd been following him. Just the Ovaro, plodding along, shaking its head to shed the rain.

When they got to the crest of the pass, Fargo steered the wagon into the pines and boulders sheathing the trail. The rain poured as hard as ever, shotgun blasts of thunder rocking earth and sky in unison, lightning flashing like sparks from a blacksmith's forge. Even the Ovaro, normally a levelheaded beast, gave an occasional nicker at the tempest's blasts, and dropped its tail between its legs, looking vaguely around for cover.

The Trailsman grabbed his rifle and led the women up the sloping knob of the pass. The crest was a broad, uneven scarp stippled with low-growing spruce and firs, occasional wild mahogany shrubs, and bunchgrass tufts.

Somewhere around here, a roofed hollow—not quite a cave—opened within boulders. He'd camped there once on a previous traverse of the country, after running off a bobcat who'd called the place home. That was where he headed now, leading Harmony by the hand, Harmony in turn leading her sister, all three crouched and squinting against the blasts of wind and rain and battlelike thunder blasts.

At the crest of low ridge, Fargo stopped. Lightning flashed, for an instant limning a square hovel in the hollow below.

"A cabin!" Harmony yelled.

The Trailsman took a minute to scrutinize the place, a stout cabin set in a small clearing around shrubs and lichen-furred boulders and the stumps of the pines that now formed the vertical timbers of the cabin's walls. The roof was flat and brush-covered. A rock chimney poked skyward. No smoke issued from it, and no horses milled in the flanking lean-to stable. A ramshackle place, but it would do for a night.

"Come on!"

Fargo jerked Harmony along behind him as he made his way down the low rocky ridge and crossed the clearing to the cabin's timbered door. As the girls waited, hunched behind him, he rammed the Henry's butt against the door twice.

Hearing nothing within, he tripped the leather latch, shoved the door wide, and aimed the rifle inside. The cabin was small enough—a single room with a rock hearth, a single cot, a rough table, a chair, and some shelves made from packing crates—to tell in a second the place was deserted.

He shoved the girls inside, then grabbed the door handle. "Go on and get dried off. If there's wood, build a fire."

He closed the door and jogged back to the wagon, keeping a sharp eye out for interlopers. When he'd unsaddled the Ovaro, unhitched the mule, and picketed both animals in some sheltering rocks and tall trees, he grabbed an armful of supplies from the wagon and went back to the cabin. He couldn't see any smoke because of the rain, but he could smell burning pine on the wind. He threw the door open. A small fire built of kindling scraps crackled in the grate.

"We'll need more wood." Charity's voice shook. Fargo slid his gaze to the right. The girls sat side by side on the cot, bare feet on the knobby earthen floor. A single thin blanket was all that covered them both, revealing nearly as much flesh as not.

"There ain't but a few sticks in the box," Harmony said, elbows tight to her sides, leaning toward the fire. Their soaked clothes were draped across the table.

"I'll take a gander."

Fargo tossed a burlap bag onto the cot beside them, then went back out and looked around the clearing. Finding split wood stacked in the lean-to—the cabin was probably a frequent overnight stop for an itinerant fur trapper—he grabbed an armload and hauled it back to the cabin.

Opening the door suddenly, he caught Harmony standing sideways to the small fire, running an end of a blanket she'd found in the gunnysack down the inside of her raised right thigh. The rest of the blanket had slipped off her shoulders to gather about her waist. Her pale breasts were provocatively silhouetted by the umber fire behind her. She glanced at Fargo. A faint smile quirked her lips.

On the cot, holding the blanket taut to her breasts and thighs, Charity whipped her head toward Fargo and gasped. "A gentleman would knock before enter-ing."

Fargo chuckled wryly as he came in, soaked to the gills, water sluicing off his hat brim, and kicked the door closed. He dropped the wood in the plank-board box beside the hearth.

When he'd built up the fire, he returned to the wagon for more gear, and got a pot of beans cooking over the flames. While the girls lounged together on the cot as the cabin grew warm, Fargo slipped out of his wet shirt and boots and sat before the fire, a tin cup of whiskey in his hand, a fresh-rolled quirley in his teeth, bare feet propped on a chair.

The rain had lightened to a drizzle. The thunder and lightning had faded altogether. Outside, water gurgled in gulleys and through the folds between rocks.

"Your pants are soaked, too, Skye," said Harmony from the cot. "Go ahead and take 'em off. We won't look—will we, sis?"

"Harmony!"

"The poor man's soaked clear through, Charity. He'll catch his death of cold!"

Fargo took a deep drag off the cigarette, blew smoke at the fire, and ended the argument. "I been wet before. I'll be wet again. This fire's dryin' me just fine."

He chuckled and glanced at the two girls curled together upon the narrow cot, sharing a cup of hot coffee smoking on a nearby chair. "Wouldn't want to give you ladies restless dreams tonight."

They both curled their noses at him. Fargo winked, chuckled, and sipped the whiskey.

Later, the rain stopped altogether, and the clouds scudded south, uncovering stars as bright as the se-quins on a queen's gown. Dried by the fire, fortified by beans, coffee, whiskey, and tobacco, Fargo strolled around outside, checking the mule, the Ovaro, and the wagon. All were unharassed, both animals contentedly grazing, relieved by the storm's passing.

The Trailsman stared along the trail curving downhill through the rocks and black pine columns, water still trickling through the new runnels it had carved. No sign of the shadow riders. Damn. Had he really seen them? If he and the girls were being trailed, why didn't their trackers attack?

Fargo thought it over.

No doubt they were waiting for him and the girls to clear open ground tomorrow in the slow-moving wagon. When they crossed the broad valley the mountain men had dubbed Pilgrim's Pass, they'd be as easy to pick off as ducks on a millpond.

Fargo turned away from the trail, gathered more wood from the lean-to, and built a small coffee fire at the base of a scarp. When he'd left the cabin, the girls were asleep. After the storm, they needed their beauty rest. He'd sleep out here and keep night watch.

When the coffee was beginning to hiss and sputter, Fargo climbed the scarp above it, north of the cabin, and hunkered down in the rocks with his rifle. He poked his hat back and ran his hawk eyes across the night, noting every form and every shadow.

He'd had two cups of coffee, and a distant hoot owl was hooting him heavy-lidded, when a click and a low squawk rose behind him. He turned.

Within the cabin's black shadow, another shadow moved. The squawk and click again—the door closing and latching.

Bare feet padded quietly across the damp ground, softly crunching gravel. Fargo's coffee fire was too low to reveal the figure until it had scuttled up close to the base of the scarp. Harmony's blond hair shone soft yellow in the flickering flames. She held several blankets around her shoulders. Her legs were bare beneath her knees.

She raised her face toward the scarp's crest. Her high feminine voice called softly, "Skye?"

He kept his own voice low. "Go back to sleep."

She shifted her shoulders, brushed the back of a hand across her cheek. "I can't sleep."

"I'm fresh outta bedtime stories."

He couldn't tell for sure from this distance, but he thought her lips curved in a smile. It was a chilly night, the air still damp from the storm, but she lowered the blankets down her arms until both pert breasts bobbed free. "Charity took some sleeping powder. It'd take a cannon to wake her."

Fargo stared down at her. His annoyance at the distraction was gradually tempered by a twitching and warming in his loins.

He glanced down the trail. No sounds. No movement. The men shadowing him were probably all snuggled up in their soogans, as wrung out by the storm as Fargo was.

Fargo turned back to the girl, her oval face staring up at him, blankets twisted about her waist. The Trailsman chuffed and pushed himself to his feet. One of these days, a pretty girl was going to be the death of him. Most likely that one down there.

Feeling like a Christian thrown into the lion's hole, Fargo started down the scarp.

12

When Fargo made the final leap to the ground and stood before the girl, she stared up at him, a devilish smile curling her lips, flashing in her eyes. She looked like a queen who'd summoned companionship with a song, knowing the poor peasant before her had had no choice but to come.

"You know me too damn well," he snarled, anger flaring in his cheeks.

She pooched her lips together and raised the blanket across her breasts. "I'm chilly!"

Fargo leaned his rifle against a rock, then turned to her, ripping the blankets from her hands. She gave a startled gasp. He dropped the blankets atop his own by the fire, then stood before her, running his eyes across her lithe, pale body, feasting on her as he unbuckled his cartridge belt. He dropped the gun and belt to the ground beside his saddle.

"Chilly, hell." He began unbuttoning his tunic, slitting his eyes at her. "You never been cold a night in your life."

She giggled. "Why should I be?"

"I ain't arguin'."

When he'd stripped down to nothing but his hat,

she stepped toward him and swiped the hat from his head. She laughed quietly. She sobered as she ran her eyes across the hard slabs of his chest and biceps and corded forearms, then down his flat belly to his jutting member, the swollen tip of which tickled her belly button.

Goose bumps rose instantly across her shoulders and down her arms. Her thighs turned hot and soft as summer mud, and her breath came short.

Fargo gently closed his hands around her arms, leaned down, and kissed her softly, sucking at her lips, entangling his tongue with hers. She groaned and dug her fingers into his biceps.

He grabbed her brusquely and tipped her head back, closing his mouth over her supple lips. They kissed for a long time, Harmony groaning and grunting, before he picked her up in his arms, stepped to the fire, and dropped to one knee. He eased her down on the blankets, then knelt over her, lowered his head to her chest, and suckled each nipple in turn, until both stood erect from the small, pink areolae. As she fondled his stiffly bobbing member, he kissed her belly, ran his lips and hands down her thighs.

Her hands rubbed and pulled; then she rose up on her elbows and closed her lips over the swollen, purple head, working him into a rage.

His breath rose sharply, the back of his neck turning hot as a blacksmith's forge. He nudged her back down to the blankets, positioning himself between her legs. She lifted her head, a sultry smile spreading across her mouth.

"Wait."

She turned over and crawled up over his saddle until she lay across it, her round, pale butt aimed skyward. The porcelain skin glistened faintly beneath a thin sheen of sweat.

She lifted her head, turned it to one side, pressed her cheek to the ground. She snaked her right forearm under her thick, curly hair at the back of her neck, and flicked it out to the side. Her voice rose just above a whisper. "Now I'm ready, Skye."

She was. He slid into her easily, parting her thighs and butt cheeks with his hands, then leaning forward and driving into her with a savage, breathy groan.

She lifted her head sharply, hair flying. "Ah, God!"

"Shhh!"

He pulled out, thrust forward. She snapped her head up to yell, but before she could get out much more than a squeak, he cupped his hand over her mouth, muffling the scream. He rode her in that fashion, hand over her mouth, thrusting fast and deep, checking his own grunts to keep from waking Charity. Beneath him, Harmony writhed and shook her head, giggling and expelling muffled screams through his fingers, thrusting her butt up to meet him at the beginning of every plunge.

The fire was nearly dead before, spent, he collapsed on top of her. After a while, he turned onto his side, and their bodies spooned together, his dwindling member nestled against her warm, slick butt.

She thrust the back of her head against his face, her silky, swirling hair falling over his eyes and nose, and he could smell the faint lavender scent of her soap. She curled an ankle around his, positioned his arm under her cheek, gave a satisfied grunt, heaved a deep, relieved sigh, and promptly fell asleep.

He didn't know how much time had passed before something woke him. He lifted his head. She groaned and shivered. The fire was out. The cold air pressed against him.

Abruptly, a shadow moved before him. As he reached blindly for his pistol, a heavy boot was hurled deep into his belly.

He heard his own agonized groan as if it had been expelled by someone else. He flopped onto his back, bringing his knees to his belly, trying to suck wind down his throat.

Clouds had again covered the moon, so it was dark as pitch. Before him, a large, bearlike silhouette crouched over Harmony. The naked girl screamed as she was jerked to her feet, blond hair flying. Heels scuffed and a man grunted, breathing heavily through his nose. As Fargo began to get some air down his throat, he smelled the fetor of rancid sweat and bear grease mixed with wood smoke and dank buckskin.

The shadowy figures, one with long blond hair swirling and bobbing atop it, receded into the darkness, heading toward the creek.

Grunting, holding one hand to his bruised ribs, the Trailsman climbed to his feet. He looked vaguely around for his pistol or rifle but couldn't see either one in the darkness. Neither would do him any good, anyway, unless he wanted to risk shooting the girl.

He scrambled forward, no longer aware of being naked, fury burning deep within him. He ran in the direction the two figures had gone, keying in on Harmony's cries, hurling himself headlong through the brush lining the creek. Branches whipped his legs and arms, and gravel gouged his feet, but he was only vaguely aware of the abrasions. The two figures, one larger than the other, appeared before him.

"No!" Harmony screamed as the man half dragged her into the water, apparently intending to cross the creek.

He lost his grip on her arm. Harmony went down, hands splashing water at the edge of the creek.

Grunting angrily, the big man crouched to grab her arm. "Git yur ass—"

He didn't finish the sentence before Fargo was on him, lowering his head and bulling into the man's left shoulder. Fargo stood over six feet tall and weighed around two hundred pounds. He was running full-out.

But Harmony's attacker was so big that Fargo felt he'd run into a tree.

The man fell into the creek with an angry roar. Water splashed up around him and Fargo, who rolled over the man's right shoulder and dug his hands into the creek's rocky bed for purchase.

His own right shoulder, which had connected with the big man's left, barked with the sharp pain running up and down his arm. Fargo shook his head and pushed himself to his feet, the icy water sluicing off his chest and arms. He looked up. The big man had gained his own feet and was trudging through the shin-deep creek, his fists balled at his sides, toward Fargo.

The Trailsman's keen eyes had adjusted, but the towering black pines flanking the big man concealed most of his features. Fargo got only an impression of his size—a good six-feet-five—and a glimpse of heavy shoulders stretching a beaded hide tunic, and a long salt-and-pepper beard. A fist came up. Fargo bolted right. His bare foot slipped off a rock, and the heavy haymaker glanced off his right cheekbone.

The Trailsman flew straight back in the water, the back of his left shoulder smacking a half-submerged stone.

The man's voice boomed above the creek's rush. "I'll teach you to mess in my affairs, ye damn snipe!"

He reached down, grabbed Fargo by one arm, and jerked him half out of the water. With his free hand, the big man shaped a fist. He was driving it forward when Fargo slammed his right knee into the man's groin.

"Owwwww!" the big man bellowed, grabbing his crotch and loosing his grip on Fargo's arm.

The Trailsman scrambled back to his feet. Teeth gritted, he splashed toward the big, raging man kneeling in the bubbling stream, clutching his wounded balls. Fargo stopped before the man, spread his feet a little more than shoulder width apart, bent forward, and rammed his foot twice against the man's right cheek and temple.

Such blows would have killed many, incapacitated most. This man only jerked back as if slapped, shook his head, threw his head back, and loosed another enraged cry at the dim stars.

He scissored his right leg against Fargo's ankles, cutting the Trailsman's feet out from beneath him. Fargo hit the stream on his right shoulder, more pain lancing him deep and igniting starbursts behind his eyes.

When the bursts abated, he saw the big man standing over him, hatless and soaked, water beading off his buckskins. Vagrant light flashed off the long, thick blade in his hand. Crooked teeth shone dimly as he spread his furry lips back from his mouth, grinning.

"Teach you!" the man grunted. "Gonna teach you *good*!"

He took a step toward the Trailsman, raising the knife in his fist, blade canted down for a deep, killing stab.

A pistol popped dully.

The big man flinched, raised his right arm defensively. A girl shouted something the Trailsman, whose ears rang incessantly, couldn't make out. The pistol popped again. The slug spanged off a rock several feet away. Another plunked into the stream with a small splash.

The big man cursed, stumbled away from the Trailsman, and almost fell. He recovered as the pistol popped again. He shouted a curse and ran, his moccasined feet plunging and splashing water, big arms swinging, long hair swaying from side to side across his broad shoulders.

He gained the creek's opposite bank and disappeared in the brush, gone.

"Skye!"

Fargo, reclining on his side, turned toward the camp

side of the creek. A slender naked figure moved toward him, slogging through the water, blond hair dancing about her face. Harmony held Fargo's long-barreled .44 straight down before her in both hands.

"Are you all right, Skye?"

Fargo shuttled another glance to the opposite side of the creek. Slowly, wincing, feeling as though he'd just wrestled a grizzly bear in the back of a small farm wagon, he pushed himself to his feet.

He sighed. "Holy shit."

The girl flung her arms around his waist and buried her face in his chest. "Oh, God!"

"It's all right," Fargo said, taking the gun from her hand. "You're all right."

"Who *was* that?"

Smoothing the girl's hair against the back of her head, Fargo cast another glance toward the shrubs into which the big man had disappeared. He lifted a shoulder. "Bogey man?"

He took the girl's hand and led her back to the camp. He looked around. No sign of Charity.

"That girl can really sleep," Fargo quipped as he wrapped several blankets over Harmony's shoulders.

"She takes sleeping powders for her nerves. She's slept through whole gunfights in Papa's saloon."

Shivering, Fargo led the blonde to the cabin and opened the door. "You get some sleep."

She turned to him, frowning. "What're you gonna do, Skye? Suppose he comes back? Suppose there's more—"

Fargo pressed a finger to her lips, shushing her. "That's what I aim to find out. You sleep now. I'll keep an eye out. Don't worry."

She rose up on the tips of her toes, kissed him, then turned and ducked into the cabin.

When Fargo had dried himself with his blankets, he dressed and hitched his cartridge belt and .44 to his waist. He built the fire up and started a fresh pot of coffee. He had no idea who the attacker had been. A mountain man, certainly, but whether he was a part of the same group Fargo had seen trailing them earlier, the Trailsman had no idea.

A big son of a bitch. Fargo felt like he'd been trampled by a bull buffalo. He was bound to feel even worse come morning.

Feeding fresh shells to his Henry while sitting on a log near the creek, he castigated himself for his carelessness.

"Ruttin' when I should've been keepin' my eyes skinned. When will I ever learn?"

He chuckled, but there was little mirth in it.

Yes, sir, these two fillies were bound to be the death of him yet . . . and he'd have no one to blame but himself. . . .

13

The misty dawn light hung like fog over the forest as the Trailsman set his right boot down quietly in the damp pine needles and sidled up to a fir tree. He squeezed his rifle in his hands and held his breath to listen.

Pine smoke touched his nostrils. He'd seen an orange pinprick of light earlier from atop one of the scarps surrounding the cabin. He'd grabbed his rifle and headed down the hill afoot so to make as little noise as possible.

The light was no doubt a breakfast fire.

The mountain man's? The men he'd seen shadowing him and the girls?

Fargo intended to find out.

No sounds but the faint scratch of burrowing creatures in the fallen leaves and needles. Earlier, he'd heard several coyotes, but even they were quiet now.

The pine scent was stronger now than before he'd angled farther left of the trail. He saw no more orange flickers amidst the dark pine columns, but the smell told him he was getting close to the bivouac.

He cat-footed forward, moving fluidly down the hill, zigzagging around the pines, firs, currant thickets, and mossy scarps and boulders. He'd left the girls asleep in the cabin. Not a good idea, leaving them alone, but he couldn't very well drag them along. Light as they were, those two would make as much noise as two grizzly bears in a doll shop.

Soundlessly, Fargo traversed a hollow about a half mile below the cabin, then crept up a wooded shoulder and hunkered down behind an uprooted aspen. The pine smoke was visible now—frothy white puffs rolling toward him, about eight feet above the forest floor. Ghostlike. Gray as soiled sheets.

Fargo peered over the aspen's bear-scarred trunk, but saw no sign of the flame. The smoke was thicker, though, its source about twenty feet ahead.

He rose and made for the smoke, keeping a pine between him and its source. Still no sounds but a few birds beginning to chirp as the shadows receded. From somewhere rose the thin, tinny gurgle of a spring.

The Trailsman paused behind the pine, took a breath, then stepped quickly but quietly out from behind it, loudly ramming a shell into his Henry's chamber and setting his boots down firmly, shoulder width apart.

The lever's metallic snarl echoed in the dense, damp silence.

Fargo leveled the Henry's barrel at the slight clearing before him, where white smoke gushed from a rock ring. There was little else but the ring. A few vegetable and fruit tins scattered about. Cigarette butts. Boot prints. Near a puddle of recently dumped coffee was a bullet patch and some spilled gunpowder. The fire had been smothered with a few handfuls of dirt, but there'd been enough wood left on it to resurrect a fugitive flame.

Thus the brief fire Fargo had seen from the scarp near the cabin.

He strode cautiously around the encampment. Four men had camped here. Four horses had been tethered a ways off in the trees, near the spring he'd heard. Judging from the prints and the coffee puddle and the unsuccessfully doused fire, they'd left here under an hour ago.

Not likely they were mountain men. No moccasin prints, and mountain men rarely burdened themselves with canned goods. They didn't normally roll cigarettes, either, preferring pipes instead.

Fargo tracked the shod horse prints toward the trail. He'd taken only a few steps, however, before his heart turned a somersault.

The girls!

He lowered the Henry, leaped a deadfall, and pumped his arms and legs as he hotfooted back the way he'd come. *Thump-thump, thump-thump!* His boots pounded the turf, his own hard breaths resounding in his ears. He was in good enough shape that his lungs didn't burn and his thighs didn't ache inordinately until he was about a hundred yards from the top of the scarp. Then his speed started to die, his heart pounding painfully, blood rushing in his ears.

Way too damn much tobacco.

His thighs squealed complaints, but he pushed on, imagining both girls dragged kicking and screaming out of the cabin, thrown over the backs of horses, being galloped away. . . .

Three-Gun Pete's coffin dragging along behind, bouncing over every rut and hummock . . .

"Mr. Fargo, what on earth?"

At the cabin's right front corner, Fargo stopped abruptly, boots skidding a little in the damp gravel, his breath raking his lungs and throat like sandpaper. Charity stood before him, a few feet from the front door, a blanket over her shoulders, a comb and brush in her hand. Behind her, Harmony hunkered over the fire, adding sticks to a fledgling blaze. She, too, regarded Fargo with fear and surprise.

"What is it, Skye?" she asked, her back tensing. "Bear?"

The Trailsman looked around the clearing nestled in the rocks and towering pines. Only the girls were here. Somewhere behind him, a hawk shrieked. Otherwise, the air was so quiet that Fargo could hear the Ovaro and the mule munching oats in the trees to his right.

The wagon! Three-Gun!

Fargo dashed into the trees where he'd parked the wagon. The Ovaro gave a startled whinny as Fargo barreled through the brush, past the horse and the mule, and stopped beside the wagon. The tarp was still in place, its stays slipknotted to the iron eyes.

Fargo removed one stay, pried up a corner, and peered into the wagon box. The coffin was still there, wedged between trunks and burlap bags. He wrinkled his nose. Old Three-Gun was beginning to smell like dead pantry rats.

He secured the stay and turned to see Harmony and Charity standing before him, side by side, fear in their eyes.

Fargo shrugged, his face warming, feeling abashed. "I reckon I'm gettin' right skittish. Everything's fine."

"Look at your face!" Charity moved toward him and touched a hand to his battered right cheek. "What happened?"

Fargo glanced at Harmony, whose face colored, her eyes silently commanding him to lie. She wore a flannel robe, and her hair was down. Pretty as ever. Not a mark on her.

Fargo saw no reason to get Charity worked up about the mountain man. They had enough to worry about. Besides, it might be tough to explain what Fargo and Harmony were doing outside together, and why Fargo had let his guard down.

"I was scrambling around the rocks last night," he

said with a self-deprecating grunt. "Lost my footing and slipped. It'll teach me to change into my moccasins when I get the urge to play ape."

Charity glanced at Harmony, who gave her sister a guileless smile, then quickly shuttled her glance to Fargo. "Any sign of the riders from yesterday, Skye?"

"Found where they camped. Not much more." Fargo brushed past the girls, heading for the fire. "We'll just have coffee here. When I'm sure we're not bein' shadowed, we'll stop and warm some beans."

"In the name of all that's good and decent, Mr. Fargo, I hope you didn't get those marks on your face scrambling down the rocks to get to my sister."

It was midmorning. They'd been on the trail only a couple of hours, but this was the fourth time he'd had to halt the wagon so the girls could answer nature's call. Fargo had to remember to ration the coffee. Harmony was hunkered down in some rocks about thirty yards down the grassy hill to their right, and it was just Fargo and Charity sitting the driver's box, waiting.

Now he turned to the brunette, slitting one eye. "Huh?"

"I woke up in the middle of the night for just an instant, and I could have sworn that Charity wasn't inside the cabin. In fact, I now recall hearing her giggle *outside*."

"What makes you think she wasn't responding to another blast of nature's horn? You girls tend to do so often enough. Maybe, on her way back to the cabin, she was giggling at my wit."

"She got up this morning looking . . . strange. Possibly guilty?"

"Maybe I told a dirty joke."

"I hope that's the only dirty thing you did last night."

Fargo grinned.

"What's so funny?" Charity asked.

"I think you're jealous."

"Not that old saw!"

Fargo leaned toward her and kissed her on the mouth. She recoiled at first, placing her hands firmly against his chest and arm. In seconds, her hands relaxed. The fingers of her right hand dug gently into his left bicep. A lock of her auburn hair wisped against his cheek.

Fargo pulled away. "There. Maybe that'll tide you over till we can get serious."

Charity's eyes blazed, and her mouth opened, but she said nothing. Her breasts heaved within the lime green blouse, pushing at the black bone buttons. She reached up with her right hand and swept the lock of hair behind her ear.

Footfalls rose. Fargo glanced downhill. Harmony was walking out from behind the rock, skirt bunched in her hands. She was barefoot as usual and was watching the ground closely for prickly pear and goatheads.

Charity glanced at her sister. The brunette's face had bleached, but two small red splotches adorned the nub of each cheek.

Catching her breath and finding her tongue, she pursed her full red lips but kept her voice low. "I wish you'd stop doing that."

Fargo grabbed the reins, grinning. "Nah, you don't."

"Everything all right?" Harmony asked as she climbed the wagon wheel, blond curls bounding across her shoulders.

"Me and your sister were just discussing ways we could cut down on the nature stops." When Harmony was seated beside her sister, who'd scooted stiffly next to Fargo, he flicked the reins against the mule's back. "Tomorrow morning, one cup of coffee apiece."

"You can't do that, Skye!" Harmony complained.

"Just did."

He turned and whistled for the Ovaro. When the pinto was strolling parallel with the wagon, Fargo handed the wagon's reins to Charity. "I'm gonna scout our backtrail. Watch for washouts. Last time I was through here after a rain, there were plenty."

"Don't worry, Mr. Fargo," Charity said as Fargo leaped onto the pinto's back. "I'm sure we'll manage without you just fine."

Taking up the reins, he gave a snort, turned the horse off the trail, and gigged it into a gallop back the way they'd come, the damp ground still giving up little dust.

He rode for a mile, carefully scanning the terrain near and far, holding his Henry across his saddle bows. When he'd seen no sign of anyone pursuing the wagon, he rode in the wagon's direction until the rattling, gray contraption was visible about a half mile ahead, gleaming in the Rocky Mountain sunshine, in a sage-stippled fold in the hills.

He turned the Ovaro left of the trail and climbed a steep rocky hill. He paused where the wild mahogany and rabbitbrush turned to piñon pines, and dug around in his saddlebags for his spyglass. He directed the glass along his backtrail, shielding the lens from the sun with his right hand.

Nothing but sun-blasted, rock-studded hills and pine slopes. He turned his head toward the wagon and frowned. Harmony was pointing south. Staring in the same direction, Charity stiffened with alarm and gave the harness ribbons a fierce shake, gigging the mule into a trot.

Fargo shuttled his own gaze in the same direction the girls had looked. Less than a mile away, four black-clad riders sat dun horses on a low, grassy ridge at the base of a higher, pine-covered shelf. Raising the spyglass, Fargo saw that all four were well armed and stiff backed, chatting casually as they turned their heads slowly, following the wagon with their eyes.

The hairs on Fargo's neck pricked in acknowledgment. The men he'd seen yesterday during the rainstorm.

No question they were following Fargo and the girls. There'd be no outrunning them on their long-legged steeds. Maybe he'd better wander over and have a chat, find out what they were after. . . .

The thought had no sooner passed through his brain than he heard a distant, jarring rattle. He turned toward the wagon. Charity had gigged the mule into a gallop. The wagon bounced and jerked along the rutted trail, at times fishtailing, Harmony gripping the seat as her blond hair flew back in the wind, shining in the late-summer sunlight.

Over and over, the girls jerked horrified gazes toward the black-clad riders, who remained atop the ridge, their horses idly cropping grama grass and swishing their tails. Specks of white shone where the riders amused grins stretched.

"Fool woman!" Fargo barked, reaching back to drop the spyglass into the saddlebags. "Ease up. You're not gonna outrun anything but *good horse sense!*"

He'd barely gotten the bag fastened when he hoorahed the pinto into an instant gallop, flying down the hill toward the trail. He didn't deadhead for the trail, but angled toward it, trying to chew up as much ground as possible between him and the wagon—at the risk of breaking the stallion's leg on a hidden rock or gopher hole.

When he caught up to those girls, he was going to sear several layers of flesh from their pretty asses with his quirt!

Ahead, the wagon dropped over a hill line.

"Come on, pinto," Fargo barked in the horse's ears. "Let's chew some ground!"

The horse bounded over the brow of the hill line, plunging down the other side. Fargo's chest tightened as he stared over the pinto's bobbing head.

Fifty yards away, the steeply descending trail curved left. The trail was washed out, deeply rutted and mud scalloped. Unable to make the turn in the deep, slick mud and with the wagon barreling down the hill behind it, the mule had missed the curve.

It careened straight down the hill toward a wide gash in the dun prairie and lime green rabbitbrush.

Fargo couldn't see what lay beyond the cut. Probably the west fork of the Ute River, swollen by runoff from last night's storm. When the mule plunged into it—as it was giving every indication of doing—the wagon would be pummeled to matchsticks, and the women along with it.

"Ah, shit!"

With a poignant sense of falling, knowing that the only way to catch up to the wagon was if the stallion suddenly sprouted wings, Fargo put his head down and ground his spurs against the Ovaro's sweat-lathered flanks. Above the loud thuds of the stallion's shod hooves, he could hear the girls screaming. Both peered over their shoulders, casting horrified, beseeching gazes behind.

Fargo grimaced. "Ah, shit."

The mule dropped from sight, pulling the girls and the wagon after it.

The screams grew shrill, then died. They were replaced by an enormous crackling and pounding and the cannonlike boom of a large object plunging into water.

14

"Well, it's all over now but the flower gatherin'," Fargo told himself as he stopped the horse at the edge of the cut.

Nausea nearly overwhelming him, he looked down.

The arroyo was filled with brick red rainwater no doubt washing down from the higher peaks. It was a swirling, raging torrent, and nearly straight down from the cut, half-submerged and bobbing like a cork in a mud puddle, lay the wagon.

Apparently the mule lay somewhere beneath the wreckage, having shattered its skull on one of the several boulders peeking up from the floodwaters—one that looked as though a bucket of red paint had been tossed on it. The wagon slid slowly along with the current, which had already taken the steamer trunks, carpetbags, and other paraphernalia and was shunting them off downstream.

Fargo picked out two heads amidst the wreckage. Two sets of arms flailed against the current. The screams and pleas sounded like little more than bird chirps against the water's roar. Both girls worked to keep their heads above the water while sliding horrified glances at their father's coffin.

The pine box was rafting through a riffle between two boulders. As it hit the bottom of the rapids, it nearly upended before the current grabbed it and sluiced it on down the twisting, broiling stream—and out of Fargo's field of vision.

"Those cats're damn near outta lives," Fargo groused as he doffed his hat and kicked out of his boots.

He tossed down his gun belt and slipped out of his buckskin pants and shirt. The clothes would encumber him in the river. Clad in only his wash-worn balbriggans, he took two long strides to the edge of the cut.

He looked down. A good seventy-foot drop. The girls had made it, but then, they had to be immortal. Deadly but lovely demons Ol' Scratch had sent to bedevil hot-blooded men like the Trailsman.

"Watch my duds, hoss," he told the pinto regarding him with black-eyed skepticism, twitching its ears.

Fargo pinched his nose closed, flung out his free arm, and stepped over the lip of the cut. He dropped so quickly that his voice box was nudged against his tonsils by his stomach. Blood rushed to his ears, threatened to blow off the top of his head.

The river enveloped him in a cold, wet blanket. He sank straight down, scraped his right foot on a rock, and pushed off the muddy bottom with his left foot. He hadn't needed to. The current instantly grabbed him, flung him to the surface, and twirled him downstream.

He spit water from his mouth, ignoring the burn of the grit in his nose. He was facing upstream. The wagon had apparently ripped loose of the mule and was tumbling toward him in pieces. He flung aside a cracked wheel and used the momentum to turn himself.

Downstream, the girls glided over dirty yellow rapids. Both fought toward the opposite shore, stretching

114

their arms out but keeping their heads above the water. They were gaining ground on the stream. Charity even seemed to have won the battle, and was wading toward the rocks and piñons along the bank, her dress clinging to her like lime green paint, black hair basted to her back.

"Papa!"

Harmony's cry turned Charity back toward the river. She shaded her eyes with a hand. "Let him go!"

Fargo tried to steer toward Harmony but quickly discovered he was fighting the current for no reason. It was taking him toward her, though in a roundabout way, bouncing him off several rocks jutting their crenelated heads above the foam.

Before he knew it, Charity stood on a sandy crescent of shore fifteen yards to his right. She stared at him, moving her lips, but his ears were half-submerged, so he didn't hear anything but the water's slobbering gurgle.

Charity pointed downstream. Harmony was a good fifty yards away. Her head and thrashing arms disappeared around a bend to the right, and she was gone.

Fargo let the current throw him toward her, and in less than thirty seconds he was shooting around the same right-curving dogleg. The canyon opened slightly. Rocks and sandbars fingered into the water from both walls. Harmony had grabbed a square rock on the left side of the river. She clung to it and glanced toward him, eyes etched with fear and exhaustion.

She screamed something he couldn't hear. The current ran him toward her. He grabbed a rock ten feet away from the girl, digging his fingers into the stone's slick, uneven surface, ramming his foot against another submerged stone to his right.

"Climb out of here!" Fargo shouted to Harmony.

She shook her head, turned her face downstream, and pointed. *"Papa!"*

Beyond her about thirty feet, the coffin had hung up on some rocks, half-wedged between two. It looked like a wood sliver bouncing around in a boiling pot.

"We have to get Papa!" Harmony screamed.

"Shit."

Fargo released the rock and let the current take him to the girl. He rammed his left foot against her stone, positioning himself directly behind her. As the current clawed at him, like cables drawing him downstream, he reached under the water and got a firm grip on Harmony's ass. Somehow he'd gotten his hand up under her dress. It was her bare, wet bottom he clutched as he lifted her up over the rock she clung to.

She gave a surprised, indignant shriek.

Fargo gave her a final thrust, and she fell forward onto the shore.

He dragged his hand out of her skirt and kicked off the rock. The current gave him a spin and swept him toward the coffin. There was a deep pool between him and the casket, and he sank low in the water, so that only his eyes and nose were above the surface.

The current gave the coffin a hard nudge, turning it just right and shooting it out between the two rocks it had been wedged between. Fargo cursed, but underwater it was only bubbles, and then he was bounding over the rapids in the coffin's wake, about ten feet behind it.

When he rose from the eddy at the bottom of the rapids, he spied the coffin caught in the same eddy, and flung his right hand toward it.

His fingers closed over the hide handle protruding from one end. As he and the coffin drifted forward into the current, Fargo kicked for the left shore, tugging the box along behind. He struggled into a V between rocks and slung his left hand up, grappling for purchase. His hand slipped off the slick sandstone and the floating coffin, pulling him half around to face the river, which tried to pull him back into the current.

He grunted, spitting water, and flung his hand again at the overhanging rock.

A hand closed over his wrist, and squeezed.

Eyes widening, Fargo jerked his head up. A bearded face stared down at him, lips spread to reveal a mouthful of tiny tobacco brown teeth, several of which appeared sharpened to razor points. The man's eyes were a dull gray, and, while his long, untidy hair was blond as a Viking's, they were almond shaped as those of a Chinese.

With Fargo's right wrist firmly clenched in his enormous gloved hand, the man bunched his lips and rose up on his knees, lifting Fargo half out of the clawing, clinging stream. The Trailsman kept his other hand on the coffin handle. The stranger pulled Fargo far enough up the rock that he could gain his own handhold while hitching up a knee. Behind him, the coffin nudged the rock with a splintering bark and scrape.

As Fargo struggled to maintain his hold on the coffin *and* the rock, the bearded stranger scooted closer to the river, reached down, and grabbed the coffin with both hands.

Fargo released the handle, drew his legs up, and sat back on his butt, coughing up water and sucking air into his chest. Water sluiced off him, covering the rock. His soaked balbriggans were like a thick outer layer of skin.

Before him, the bearded stranger tugged the coffin out of the river and slid it up onto the rock. The man had made the maneuver with relative ease. Not a difficult back-and-belly jog for an hombre his size. As he straightened, throwing back his head to loosen the kinks in his neck, Fargo saw that he stood just under six feet tall. His heavy, sloping belly strained his buckskin breeches and gun belt and had opened several buttons of his ratty deerskin shirt.

But he was wide as a barn door, with yoke-sized shoulders and hub-sized arms. His beard was trimmed with four small braids wrapped in small ribbons of rawhide. A mountain, without doubt. Those scarred, gnarled hands were the result of setting traplines in snowmelt for at least a decade.

He owned the same fetor as the man Fargo had fought last night—raw meat and bear grease—and for a moment Fargo wondered if he'd just met up with the same hombre.

Doubtful. This man was far shorter than the mountain man who'd visited last night's camp. That didn't mean he wasn't from the same party, however. Fargo glanced at the big Colt's Dragoon hanging off the man's beefy right thigh, heavy as a war hatchet, and wished his own .44 weren't lying atop that ridge two miles upstream.

He could have been wearing his buckskins, but without that gun and cartridge belt, he felt as naked as the day he was born.

The man grinned down at him, glancing at the coffin, his fists on his hips. But he didn't say anything. Odd behavior for a city man, but not so odd for a man who probably didn't get out much.

The Trailsman spit a stream of sand-flecked saliva into the river. "Name's Fargo."

The man shook his head, then leaned forward and opened his mouth. Fargo peered through the dark hole beyond the small black teeth. What was left of the man's tongue hung back like a small mouse in its hole.

Grinning, the man closed his mouth, straightened, gestured the Indian sign for Arapaho, and made a cutting motion across his mouth.

"Handy with knives, them Arapaho," Fargo commented.

The man chuckled, cast a puzzled glance at the coffin, returned his gaze to Fargo, and shrugged a shoulder. You didn't get far in the mountains inquiring too heavily of strangers, even strangers you'd found swimming with coffins. He turned a look over his left shoulder, where two mules were picketed in a small aspen copse, and a small fire sent thin blue smoke skyward.

The man turned back toward Fargo, and he'd just started signing *fire* and *coffee,* when a girl's voice rose from upstream. "Skye?"

Fargo glanced over his right shoulder. Harmony was bounding over the rocks along the river, arms thrown out for balance, heading toward him. Her thin cream-colored dress clung to her, revealing every curve, her pert breasts jostling like two small pears in a gunnysack.

She'd lifted her head and opened her mouth to yell again, when, seeing the stranger standing over Fargo, she closed her mouth and froze. She waved her arms to maintain her balance atop a small boulder. As she stared at the mountain man, her brows furled warily.

More softly, with a skeptical note in her voice, she said, "Skye?"

Fargo glanced up at the stranger, who stared at the girl with obvious lust in his dull gray eyes. Fargo even thought he detected drool beginning to slide out one corner of his mouth, dampening his beard. The man turned his gaze to Fargo, who admonished him with a look.

Grumbling under his breath, the man shrugged, turned, chuckled, and began ambling off toward his bivouac in the aspen copse. He limped deeply over his right hip.

When the man was halfway to the coffee fire, Harmony continued skipping across the rocks toward Fargo. The Trailsman stood, not relishing the idea of walking two miles upstream, soaked to the gills and barefoot, but he saw no other way.

Again, he was visited by the urge to paddle both girls' naked asses with his saddle quirt.

"Skye!" Harmony intoned, pressing her head against his chest and wrapping her arms around his waist. "You're alive!"

"Won't know for sure till I get some whiskey down my gullet."

She glanced around him toward the aspen copse, where the mountain man now sat by his fire, a cup in his hand, staring toward Fargo. Harmony looked up at Fargo, eyes wide. "Is that . . . ?"

"Not unless he shrank." Or got his tongue cut out sometime between now and last night, Fargo added to himself.

Spying the waterlogged pine box, Harmony pulled away from Fargo, dropped to her knees beside the coffin, and pressed her cheek against the lid. "Papa!"

Fargo cast his gaze upstream. A dark-haired hourglass figure in a clingy lime green dress was making her way toward him.

"Well, here we are—all four of us, together again." Fargo shook his head and began walking upstream, his balbriggans making wet, squawking sounds as he moved. "Ain't that sweet?"

15

Fargo left the girls with the coffin even though the lusty mountain man was near. He figured if the mountain man wanted to assault them, he could go ahead and do so. Fargo wanted to assault them both, and hold their heads under water till they stopped blowing bubbles.

Because of their dunderheaded maneuver, they were now without a wagon, a mule, and the girls' camping gear. That meant they'd have to rely on Fargo's meager stores as well as his horse.

When he'd cursed his way back to the point at which the wagon had tumbled headlong into the river—the mule and the wagon were gone, both apparently having been washed downstream—Fargo continued upstream for fifty yards, then plunged in. He swam hard against the current but still didn't gain the opposite shore until the water had swept him thirty yards down from the site of the wreck.

It was an angry, gill-soaked Trailsman who climbed the ridge barefoot, digging his toes into the slick clay bank and pulling himself up by exposed tree roots. At the top, the pinto was waiting for him, holding its head down and flicking its ears, regarding him snidely, as if to say, "What're you going to get yourself into next?"

"Shut up, horse."

The pinto whinnied and shook its head.

Fargo donned his dry clothes over the wet balbriggans, and snugged his hat on his head. It wasn't until he was wrapping his .44 and cartridge belt around his waist that he remembered the cause of this mess—the four men who'd been pursuing him and the girls.

He jerked a look back along the hill rising to a cedar-tufted ridge. Nothing but wild grass, shrubs, and the muddy ribbon of washed-out trail. No sign of the riders.

Fargo rolled a cigarette and stood, leaning against the Ovaro's right rear hip, staring along his backtrail and pondering the five men as he smoked. If they'd wanted old Three-Gun, there hadn't been a better time to make their move than when Fargo, the girls, and old Three-Gun himself were in the river.

Maybe it wasn't Three-Gun they were after.

Maybe they weren't after *anything*. Hell, maybe they just happened to be sharing the same old trace with Fargo, coincidentally heading in the same direction as the Trailsman and the girls.

Fargo took a deep, final drag off the quirley. Blowing smoke and staring at the western ridge capped with midafternoon blue sky, he shook his head. Damn curious. He field-stripped the cigarette, letting the breeze take the remaining tobacco, then hauled himself into the saddle and reined the Ovaro eastward.

When he'd found a relatively easy trail down to the river, the stallion forded without trouble, holding its grand head proudly above the current. When man and horse had gained the other side, Fargo gigged the pinto downstream.

He knew a moment's apprehension when he saw only the coffin sitting on the rock where he'd left the girls. Shuttling his gaze toward the mountain man's bivouac, he frowned. No sign of the man. Only the fire, which had doubled in size since the Trailsman had last seen it. Sitting huddled around it now, two ratty blankets draped across their shoulders and looking like two drowned muskrats, were Charity and Harmony.

Fargo spit and, brows ridged with curiosity as he looked around for the mountain man, rode over. He stopped the pinto about fifteen feet from the fire, which was banked with driftwood and stretching its flames four feet high.

"He left," Harmony said, shivering and planting one bare foot atop the other, the foot pale and pruned from the water. "He built up the fire first, beckoned us over, and rode off."

Charity brushed ashes from her cheek. Her voice shook. "At last, a gentleman in this godforsaken wilderness."

Fargo snorted and glanced at the fire, the nice stack of wood beside it. He looked around again for the mountain man. Seeing no sign of anyone, he said, "I reckon we'll spend the night here. Give you time to dry out, me time to rig a travois for your pa."

Harmony glanced up at him, crestfallen. "How're *we* gonna get to Del Norte now, Skye? Me and Charity, without the wagon?"

Fargo wanted to tell her they could walk.

They both looked miserable enough, however. He almost felt sorry for them—out here in the middle of nowhere, their father lying dead in his box by the river. What kind of future did two young ladies have—orphaned, homeless, and manless—on the frontier?

He hoped to hell they didn't turn to what most girls in similar positions turned to.

They sat before him, hunched into themselves, shivering. He reached back into one of his saddlebags, grabbed his battered coffeepot with a small pouch of beans tucked inside. He dropped the pot at the girls' feet.

"Best start some coffee. I'll ride down river a ways, see what I can find of your gear."

As he rode off, Charity's shrunken voice lifted behind him. "Mr. Fargo?"

He stopped and hipped around in his saddle.

She stared at him, then dropped her eyes demurely as she said, barely loud enough to hear above the breeze and the fire, "I'm sorry."

The Trailsman spit to one side. "What's a trip without a few travails?"

He turned forward and gigged the pinto downriver.

Fargo found no sign of the girls' steamer trunks. He did find a couple of soaked quilts hung up on rocks. With a long stick, he fished them out of the river and brought them back to the camp, where the girls were drinking coffee and not shivering quite so much, and hung them from a low aspen branch near the fire.

He spent the rest of the afternoon rigging a travois from peeled branches and rope, then fixed the coffin onto the travois, deciding to leave the box and travois a good distance from the camp. Old Three-Gun Pete was getting more than a little whiffy on the lee side.

Fargo hoped the dead gunslinger didn't lure in wolves or a grizzly during the night.

With a string and a hook baited with grasshoppers, Fargo caught a couple of good-sized red-throated trout and roasted them over the fire. He and the girls ate the fish, seasoned with salt and wild mint, while sitting around the fire and staring silently into the flames. When they'd washed the fish down with the coffee, Fargo dug a whiskey bottle from his saddlebags and held the bottle down between them.

"Anyone for a snort?"

"No, thank you," Charity said primly, hugging her knees. She'd donned her dress again and wrapped herself in a quilt, both dried by the fire, but she still looked washed-out and cold.

"You sure?" Fargo encouraged. "Warm you up."

Harmony glanced at her sister, her brows furrowed with consternation, then grabbed her empty coffee cup off a rock. She held it up to Fargo with a devilish light in her eyes. "Why not?"

Charity snapped a reprimanding look at her. "Harmony!"

"I'm cold, sis!" Harmony sipped the whiskey, then smacked her lips. "Besides, it'll help me sleep. It'd do you some good, too."

Harmony turned back to the fire, Charity watching her skeptically. Fargo nudged her shoulder with the bottle. "I ain't tryin' to loosen your corset, just tryin' to breathe some fire down your gullet."

The corner of the brunette's mouth turned down. "I suppose just a sip wouldn't hurt." She extended her cup to Fargo. "Since it's for medicinal purposes."

"The only way I use it." Fargo chuckled, splashing a dollop into the cup.

When Fargo had downed a couple shots of the whiskey himself, he corked the bottle, set it against the log he'd been sitting on, then grabbed his Henry and strode off on night patrol. A half hour later, he returned to find the uncorked bottle propped against a rock and both girls lying entangled beside the fire, snoring like farmers.

Fargo squatted down, picked up the bottle, and examined it against the flames. Not more than a shot left. He cursed, tipped back the shot, and tossed the bottle into the brush.

He shook his head and looked at the girls, spooned together like lovers. One of the quilts had come down, and Charity's full breasts, shoved up by Harmony's arm, were spilling out of her dress. The smooth, soft flesh was bronzed by the firelight—two good handfuls and more.

The Trailsman cursed and shook his head with appreciation, then wandered to the other side of the fire.

He sank down against the log, rested the Henry across his thighs, and closed his eyes.

He didn't sleep long, however. Not with the four black-clad riders lurking around. He spent most of the night patrolling the camp from the river to the chalky buttes rising in the south, catching a few winks between trips.

He returned from one such patrol just before dawn to find Harmony tossing a handful of coffee grounds into Fargo's blackened pot, her hair tangled about her head, a quilt hanging off her shoulders.

Charity was nowhere in sight.

The Trailsman frowned. "Where's your sister?"

Harmony turned to him with a start, slapping a hand to her chest. "You spooked me, Skye!"

"Where's your sister?"

Harmony turned the corners of her mouth down, abashed. "Tryin' to walk off her headache." Her eyes met Fargo's. "Why?"

" 'Cause it ain't safe to go traipsing off alone out here. Which way'd she go?"

"Downriver." Sitting back on her heels, Harmony stared in that direction, the dawn light pearling about the aspens. "Come to think of it, she *did* light out quite a while ago."

"Christ!"

Fargo ran over to where he'd picketed the stallion, quickly tacked up the mount, slid his rifle into the sheath, and swung up into the saddle.

"Stay here!" he told Harmony, and spurred the pinto into a gallop, angling toward the river hidden in the misty predawn shadows.

It didn't take him long to find the prints of Charity's canvas slippers in the dew-damp grass. He followed the tracks for a quarter mile, then checked the Ovaro down suddenly.

He leaned out from his left stirrup, frowning down at the deep grass lining the riverbank. Two horseback riders had intersected the girl's tracks, then headed downriver. The girl's slipper prints had disappeared. No sign of them. Only the two sets of unshod hoofprints.

Indians had grabbed her.

Strange, only two—Utes normally rode in packs. Fargo spurred the Ovaro ahead, trotting to keep a close eye on the sign. No point in overriding the trail, then having to backtrack.

He'd followed the trail for nearly a mile when it started curving toward a rocky cut in the low ridge left of the river. At the same time he swung the pinto toward the cut, a woman's scream echoed. Close on its heels rose a man's gleeful laugh.

A white man's husky laugh.

Fargo heeled the pinto into a gallop, angling toward the dark oval of the cut's mouth shrouded in cracked boulders and scrub brush. Swerving left of the cut, he urged the pinto up the pine-columned hill for about twenty yards. Hearing another cry from Charity, followed by more laughter, Fargo slipped out of the saddle, dropped the reins, and shucked the Henry.

He crouched and peered toward the cut, slowly levering a fresh shell into the rifle's breech.

She was crying now. The man was barking orders at her.

Taking the Henry in one hand, Fargo trotted forward, then crouched down near the lip of the cut. He laid the Henry across his thighs, doffed his hat, and lifted a look over the cut's brow.

Below lay a tongue-shaped box canyon. A small spring gurgled out from the mossy shale at the canyon's far side, dropping with a soft, unceasing splashing sound on the sand and high green grass below, forming a pool. Three horses—a claybank, a paint, and a buckskin bedecked with a wooden-framed pack and panniers—were tethered to the willows near the pool. In the middle of the canyon, the stocky mountain man who'd helped Fargo out of the river crouched on his haunches, stretching his lips back from his braided beard, showing his black teeth as he chuckled wickedly, wringing his hands together.

Before him stood Charity and the big mountain man who'd nearly pummeled Fargo senseless the night before last. The brunette was topless, her blouse lying in the grass near the spring. One ankle was tied by a long rawhide thong to a wooden stake that had been driven into the canyon's sandy soil. Somehow, she'd gotten a knife—a wide-bladed bowie with a savagely upswept tip—and she was slashing at the air before her, trying to hold the big man at bay.

The mountain of a man was naked from the waist down, wearing only a fringed and beaded deerskin tunic and several claw-ornamented necklaces, which jostled as he circled the girl, crouched like a savage, laughing, his eyes glinting feral fire. His hairless bowed legs were pale as parchment, the slablike hamstrings and quadriceps showing gunmetal blue in relief.

The huge leg muscles convulsed as he bolted toward Charity. She screamed and slashed at his chest, her big breasts jumping. He bolted back as the knife slashed through one of the rawhide thongs hanging from his neck, and a necklace fell in the grass.

Charity covered her breasts with her left arm, pointing the knife with her other hand. "I'll stab you, goddamn you! You leave me alone. You have no right to do this to me!"

As the big mountain man lowered his chin to survey the damage to his necklace, snarling and circling the girl about three feet from the end of her thong, Fargo raised the Henry. He'd planted a bead on the moving man's chest when the big man suddenly sidestepped left, putting the girl's slender, curving back between himself and Fargo.

He towered over the girl, head canted forward, chin tipped, to laugh and jeer.

"You're makin' this much too hard, missy!" The

man's voice echoed around the box canyon like cannon blasts. "Not that I mind. I like wrastlin' polecats. Me and Jedediah over there—we like to work fer it. Don't we, Jedediah?"

The tongueless mountain man clapped his hands and made incoherent grunting sounds, rising from a crouch to leap straight up in the air like a euphoric ape. Fargo adjusted the Henry's barrel, planting the bead on the big man's forehead.

The man snapped his hand forward. He grabbed Charity's wrist. The girl screamed and dropped the bowie. The big mountain man's laughter rose like thunderclaps as he jerked the girl around, turning her back to him, then lifted her in the air before him, cupping her breasts in his massive brown hands.

He held her up, kicking and screaming, like a trophy.

Fargo cursed and snapped the Henry down. He couldn't fire now without risking hitting the girl. Even a wayward shot might ricochet off one of the rocks lining the canyon.

As the stocky mountain man ran around the big man and Charity, leaping and clapping his hands and making savage animal noises, the big man carried Charity toward the back of the canyon.

"Now, watch here how it's done, Jedediah!"

Both men laughed as Charity cried and protested, kicking and flailing her arms. She was little more than a rag doll in the big man's grip, her hair flying about her head and his.

As the big man thrust Charity forward over a flat-topped boulder and ripped her skirt off, Fargo spied a way down the canyon's wall. He was moving toward it when a rock gave beneath his boot. The Trailsman dropped to his right knee. Before he knew it, he was falling forward, turning head over heels, the floor of the canyon growing vast before his wide-stretched eyes.

He hit the canyon floor with a heavy thud, the air gushing from his lungs in a single exhalation.

Far to his right, the Henry hit the sandy ground with a clattering thump.

The tongueless man squealed with excitement, jumping up and down.

The big mountain man turned. "Well, look who's come callin', Jedediah!"

16

The Trailsman lifted his head. His skull throbbed. His back ached. His ankle screamed, swelling against his boot.

"Shoot the son of a bitch, Jedediah!" barked the big mountain man, jerking a thumb at Fargo, then slapping Charity's knees apart and ripping her pantaloons with one savage swipe of his hand.

"No!" the girl screamed, kicking her naked legs and turning her face on the rock to cast a terrified, beseeching look at Fargo.

Jedediah narrowed his eyes at Fargo and started toward him slowly, crouching. The man closed his hands over the bone grips of his big Dragoon. As he began sliding the heavy iron from his holster, Fargo's own hand closed around the smooth walnut grips of his .44. Grinding his teeth, shutting out the pain, and willing the canyon to stop spinning around him, Fargo raised the pistol.

He was a moment too late.

Jedediah ratcheted back the Dragoon's hammer, closed one eye and squinted the other, sighting down the barrel, and fired. Smoke puffed and flames geysered. At the same time the heavy slug plunked into the sod two inches from Fargo's right ear with a heavy *flumppp*, Fargo squeezed his .44's trigger.

The gun popped.

In the willows, one of the horses whinnied.

Still moving toward Fargo like a stalking mountain lion, Jedediah grunted as blood splashed from the center of his upper chest. Stretching his lips back from his teeth, he clapped his left hand over the wound. He half turned and dropped to his knees.

The big mountain man stepped back from Charity and turned to his wounded partner, his giant face blazing crimson. "*Goddamn you, Jedediah!*"

He wheeled toward Fargo, scowling and gritting his teeth. Fargo slid the Colt's barrel toward him, but the angle was too awkward for an accurate shot. He pushed up on his elbows, keeping his gaze glued to the big mountain man, who squared his shoulders at Fargo and moved toward him like an enraged griz, clutching the big bowie in his right fist.

"You come trompin' on the wrong fuck-fest, mister!"

The big man's hand flicked back behind his shoulder, then snapped forward. Fargo glimpsed the broad knife tumbling toward him.

He flinched right.

Winking in the sunlight angling through the pines, the huge knife whooshed past his ear and embedded itself in the ground with a resolute *sniffit-ching*!

"Skye!" Charity crouched beside the boulder, holding one arm over her breasts while arranging her skirt across her thighs.

Fargo regained a knee, aimed the .44, and fired.

The pop echoed.

The mountain man blinked as the bullet plunked into his right side. Cursing, he reached over his right shoulder, producing another knife—a fine-honed Arkansas toothpick similar to the Trailsman's own.

The man loosed a lionlike roar and, clutching the

toothpick in his right hand, put his head down and sprang toward Fargo.

Fargo squinted through the pain-fog, willing the canyon to stop spinning once more, and fired. The bullet, drilling through the mountain man's left shoulder, had no effect whatever. The man kept running, closing and yelling like an enraged bull buff flanked by a prairie blaze.

Fargo fired four more shots into the man before he so much as flinched.

Aiming with both hands, still on one knee, Fargo drilled a fourth round into the man's heart.

"Ughh!"

The mountain man dug his heels into the ground and dove toward Fargo.

The Trailsman dropped the .44 and reached up with both hands, grabbing the wrist of the hand clenching the knife, shoving it to one side as the razor-sharp tip carved a furrow across Fargo's left cheek. Fargo fell on his back, the mountain man on top of him, writhing and sputtering and grunting curses.

He tried to bring the knife back toward Fargo's throat, but the Trailsman kept both hands closed around the man's knife wrist, pinning the hand to the ground just off Fargo's shoulder. Slowly, as the blood gushed out of the man, sopping Fargo's own tunic, the man's muscles relaxed. His face fell slack.

Finally, when the man sprawled atop him, limp, Fargo rolled onto his left side, releasing the man's wrist and sliding out from beneath the heavy, bulky, half-naked body.

Charity sobbed, holding her face in her hands.

Heavily, Fargo moved toward her.

When he was ten feet from the girl, a guttural, gasping wheeze sounded behind him. He wheeled, stumbled, and nearly fell. When he'd regained his balance, he blinked with disbelief.

The blood-soaked mountain man, looking like

something rising from the dead, had climbed to one knee.

"You . . . You're gonna die . . . mixin' in my 'fairs . . ."

Fargo glanced around. His rifle lay ahead and to the left, on the other side of the canyon, half leaning against a deadfall pine. Hearing Charity muttering "Oh, God!" over and over behind him, Fargo stumbled toward the rifle.

The mountain man gained his other foot and slogged toward the rifle, on an interception course with Fargo. Increasing his speed, gritting his teeth against the pain in his head, and focusing his eyes solely on the Henry, Fargo got to the rifle three steps before the mountain man.

He crouched down, picked up the gun, and whipped around. Before he could level the barrel, the big man was on him, swiping the rifle down with an incredible chop of his left fist, and raising the Arkansas toothpick high above his head, blade down, for a killing plunge.

Charity screamed.

A hole opened in the big man's right temple—big as a saddle horn and spewing gore.

He stumbled forward, got his bare feet entangled in Fargo's, and fell forward on his face. In the lower left side of the back of his head, blood glistened around a quarter-sized bullet hole.

Only then did Fargo realize that, beneath Charity's scream, he'd heard a rifle crack. Peering up at the canyon's far rim, he saw a flat-brimmed black hat and a rifle barrel appear behind a puff of dispersing powder smoke. Two dark eyes peered down at him before the man retreated behind the ridge. A moment later, hooves thudded, dwindling as they ascended the mountain.

Branches snapped. A man chuckled softly. Then a funereal silence fell over the canyon.

The Trailsman looked back down at the unmoving

mountain man. With half his brains blown out, he wouldn't be getting up again. Fargo shifted his gaze once again to the ridge.

Who had blown them out? One of the four black-clad riders?

Fargo looked at Charity. Crouched beside the flat-topped boulder, she'd fallen silent. Her face betrayed her befuddlement and awe as she held his stare, her lower jaw hanging.

"Teach you to go walkin' off by yourself," Fargo said with a grunt.

The Trailsman helped Charity back down the box canyon, one arm around her waist, carrying his rifle in his free hand. Harmony appeared, running toward them, breathless.

"What happened?"

"Your sister attracted a bad element."

Harmony grabbed her sister's shoulders. "Charity, are you all right?"

The brunette nodded. She was bruised and battered, her hair hanging down, her clothes ripped and barely hanging on her frame, but she'd survive. She was still sobbing, and the tears ran in earnest when Harmony hugged her.

The blonde and Fargo helped Charity back toward the camp, walking slowly as Charity, having lost her slippers, was barefoot and not used to it. Fargo asked Harmony if she'd seen the four strangers dressed in black.

Harmony whipped her head toward Fargo. "I thought that's who attacked you."

Fargo looked up the pine- and slash-covered hill to the east, where the purple shadows receded as the sun climbed above the ridge. Having spied him and the girls, the Ovaro was trotting down the incline, zigzagging between pines. "They didn't attack us. They saved our bacon."

"Huh?"

Fargo explained, then asked, "How good a look did you get?"

"Just enough to know they were all dressed alike. I saw a couple faces but I couldn't really describe them."

Fargo stopped and regarded both girls gravely. "They must be after you two. Think. Where've you seen four hard-faced hombres with a fetish for black trail gear?"

They looked at each other, frowning.

Charity turned her tear-streaked face to Fargo and threw up her hands. "Nowhere!"

"You've never seen them around your old man's saloon?"

Harmony shook her head. "Never."

Fargo winced partially from frustration, partially from the tom-tom in his skull. "Damn puzzling." He grabbed Charity around the waist, threw her onto the Ovaro's hurricane deck, and tossed the reins to Harmony. Charity's torn blouse dropped off her shoulders to reveal her magnificent, red-brown-tipped breasts. In her condition, she was slow to raise the garment back over her shoulders, but Fargo tried to give the orbs only a passing glance.

"You two go on back to the camp."

As he turned and staggered back toward the canyon's narrow mouth, Harmony called, "Where're you going?"

Fargo didn't turn around as he limped along, grunting, on his sprained ankle. "Those two fur trappers weren't such bad luck, after all. They left horseflesh."

Good horseflesh, it turned out. The claybank and paint were both strong, hardy-looking horses, fully rigged out with leather saddles and bedrolls. The bedrolls were probably infested with lice and a few other things, but they'd serve their purpose. The packhorse was loaded with cooking and camping gear and even a couple of snared rabbits.

Not believing in burying men who'd tried to kill him, he left the mountain men where they'd fallen, to the scavengers, who had to eat, too. . . .

When he'd ridden the paint back to his and the girls' camp, leading the other two mounts, Fargo chucked most of the unneeded camping gear into the woods and hitched the coffin-burdened travois to the packhorse with the halter and harness ribbons he'd fashioned from rawhide and rope.

Within an hour after getting back to camp, he and the girls headed out, Harmony riding the claybank, Charity the paint. Fargo trailed the packhorse and travois on a long lead line, so Three-Gun Pete's death stench wasn't so pesky.

Even with the travois, they made good time on this, the last leg of their journey, traversing a low pass over the southwest shoulder of Starr Mountain and spending the night camped along Big Spring Creek, in the San Luis Valley.

Several times that day and the next, Fargo scouted ahead and behind, spotting Indian sign but no Indians. While he ran across shod hoofprints, there were never four all together, and, though he scoured the terrain with his spyglass, he caught no more glimpses of the black-garbed men in their flat-brimmed hats.

It was with a great light feeling that he mounted a low hill the next day around noon, and stared down the rise at the village strewn about the piñons and sage of the adobe-colored valley below. Goats bleated and pigs snorted. A baby cried. Cook fires and chimney pipes sent the smell of cooking meat to Fargo's nose. He thought he could even smell the fair-to-middling whiskey that old Rudy Belarski brewed in his well-appointed Venus Hotel and Saloon at the heart of the mud-and-adobe village.

"Well, I'll be damned," he growled around the quirley in his teeth. "We made it."

Harmony and Charity rode up on either side of him. "At last." Charity sighed.

"I didn't think we'd ever get here in one piece," said Harmony.

"Well, we did," the Trailsman said, stripping his quirley. "Now, without sounding rude, let's go plant your old man so I can get shed of you two and go find a drink. Where'd they turn his brother toe-down?"

"Papa said it was in one of the only two boothills in town," Charity said after giving the Trailsman an incriminating look, shading her eyes with a hand.

"The southwest side of town." Harmony pointed to a couple of sunbaked acres of stone and wood crosses tilting amongst the rocks and bunchgrass spilled across a butte shoulder.

Fargo clucked the Ovaro forward. "Shake a leg."

When they'd circled the town and climbed the butte, the girls dismounted and strode separately around the crosses until they found the one with their uncle's name burned into the wood. It lay near a cracked sandstone boulder and a juniper. Six feet to its right lay another, smaller, heart-shaped rock sheathed in greasewood.

"Right here's where Papa wanted to be buried," Harmony said, planting a bare foot in the dust just before the rock. She tapped her dirty foot several times, a flush rising in her cheeks and her breath coming fast. "Right here."

Fargo stood behind her. Charity was running up from another section of the boneyard, holding her hair back from her face with one hand. Her cheeks, too, were brushed apple red.

Fargo studied both girls with interest. They looked more excited than distraught. Damn peculiar. But then, nothing about this trip had been run-of-the-mill.

Maybe they were as eager as Fargo to be rid of the stinky old box of Three-Gun Pete's bones.

"I suppose I'm supposed to dig the grave." Fargo snorted with a crooked grin.

"Would you, Skye?" said Harmony. "I'd rather not get my hands all callusy, and Charity has no strength in her arms *at all*!"

Fargo snorted as he turned and strode to the horses. He retrieved his folding shovel from his saddle and, leaving the horses and fetid freight back near the cemetery's gate, tramped back to the girls. He removed his neckerchief, rolled up his shirtsleeves, unbuttoned his shirt, and started digging.

"That oughta do it," he said a half hour later, tossing the shovel on the mound of freshly dug sand, clay, and gravel beside the hole.

"I don't think that's deep enough, Skye," said Harmony. She and her sister were leaning against the rock, Charity holding a bright pink parasol over their heads. They both frowned into the hole.

"Not near deep enough," agreed Charity.

The Trailsman sleeved sweat from his brow and regarded the girls with barely contained fury. "What're you talking about?"

"That's not six feet," said Charity.

"It's not even five!" added Harmony.

"Four feet's deep enough for Three-Gun Pete," Fargo countered, hoisting himself from the hole. "Besides, I'll cover it with rocks."

When the girls assaulted him with stewing silence, Fargo glanced at them. Neither one caught his eye. They stared at the hole, poker-faced. Harmony shifted an outstretched leg slightly, so that her dress drew taut across her thigh.

"Shit," Fargo sighed, picking up the shovel and dropping back into the hole. "Two more lousy feet and I'm free at last!"

When he'd dug two more feet, he began clearing out the last of the loose gravel. His shovel nudged something that didn't feel like dirt. His brows ridged. With the tip of the shovel blade, he probed the fleck of dirty cloth tonguing up from the grave's right rear corner.

"Hope I haven't uncovered someone else's carcass," Fargo muttered, working the gravel away from the cloth.

"What?" Harmony leaned out from beneath the parasol.

"Hit somethin' that ain't dirt."

Dropping the parasol, Charity lurched forward, dropping onto her hands and knees, ass in the air, and peered into the hole. She didn't seem to care that her voluminous bosoms, bubbling down from her chest, were nearly entirely exposed by her torn, sagging blouse. "Dig it up, Mr. Fargo!"

Harmony laughed with glee. "Dig it up, Skye!"

Fargo turned to them. "What the hell's goin' on here?"

Harmony kept her eyes on the strip of burlap near Fargo's feet. "Dig it up and you'll see."

Resting on the shovel, its blade embedded in a wall of the grave, Fargo cut his eyes to each girl in turn. They stared so intently into the hole that they resembled dogs waiting for a rabbit to show from its burrow.

Fargo sighed. "What the hell have I gotten myself into now . . . ?"

He dropped the shovel blade into the hole and, muttering curses, chipped the stones and dirt away from the cloth. As the girls watched over his shoulder, practically salivating, he slowly uncovered what turned out to be a rotten wooden box, like those used for storing gun cartridges. In places, the slatted wood had broken down, exposing the burlap within.

Fargo chucked the shovel out of the hole.

"Come on, Skye," Harmony urged. "Time's awastin'."

Fargo gave her a wry look, then stooped down and wrapped his hands around the box. He had it halfway to his knees when the wood crumbled, and all three small sacks inside, roughly the size of month-old pigs, clattered to the ground. Fargo was left with two slats of rotten wood in his gloved hands. He stared disbelievingly down at the lumpy bags.

Moneybags. Coins. Had to be several thousand dollars' worth.

Through the dirt and grime on one bag he could vaguely make out two large, dark letters: U.S.

Army payroll money.

"Ah, shit."

"Oh, my God, Papa was right," Charity said breathily, hang-jawed.

"He wasn't just goin' senile in his old age," Harmony whispered as she stared down at the bags. "The money's really here!"

Fargo gave each a stern look, bunching his lips with fury. "What have you two vixens got me into?"

Somewhere behind Fargo, a horse whinnied.

A figure moved across the sun, angling a shadow across Fargo's left shoulder. "I'll tell you."

Fargo whipped his head around. A tall man in a white shirt, brocade vest, string tie, and black clawhammer coat, stared down at him from beneath the brim of his low-crowned, flat-brimmed black hat. His gray-blue eyes were as flat as a reptile's, giving the lie to the curve of his lips. In the man's right fist was a navy Colt revolver, hammer back, its brass housing glistening in the midday light.

The barrel was aimed at Fargo's face.

17

From around the boulder the girls had been sitting on, four more men strolled. Three held pistols. One held a Spencer repeater in his folded arms. He smiled down at Fargo wolfishly.

All four were dressed in black. The one nearest Fargo appeared the oldest, not to mention the most ruthless. Gray streaked his dark hair and sideburns.

"I was just a little shaver when me, Three-Gun, Karl, and the boys robbed that payroll detail down at Fort McClane," the man said, keeping his revolver aimed at Fargo's face as he squatted beside the girls and edged a glance into the hole. "Always wondered what happened to it." He chuckled. "Buried it beside ol' Karl."

Harmony and Charity had both gained their knees, regarding the black-clad strangers warily.

"Who the hell are you?" Harmony demanded, her eyes flashing fire.

The man tipped his head regally. "The Reverend Justin Lawrence Peabody the third, at your service. I'm a friend of your old man's. Leastways, I was before we split up, and your old man and Karl took off with the money. Me an' the other boys were caught.

They all died in prison, from the lead that posse of soldiers drilled into us. I did eight years. When I got out, I couldn't find hide nor hair of your pa . . . or the payroll gold. Figured he'd changed his name and spent all the money."

The "Reverend" poked the brim of his hat up with his pistol barrel and shook his head as he turned to the girls. A lock of gray-brown hair curled wetly against his forehead, dripping sweat onto his scarred nose. His jaws quivered with barely contained emotion.

"For years I scoured the frontier for that son of a bitch. Meant to kill him like I killed my own pa— slow—for ridin' us into that trap, then runnin' off on us. Then I run into the man that broke away with ol' Three-Gun and Karl. Iver Lomax. I'd figured he was dead. He was only crippled. Confined to a wheelchair. He said your old man and Karl left him in a roadhouse to heal up from his wounds. He found your old man later, learned that ol' Three-Gun had buried the money somewhere, wanted nothin' more to do with it since it's what caused Karl's death. He wanted *nobody* to have anything to do with it."

"Blood money, he called it," Charity said, staring grimly into the hole. "Cursed money."

"He found religion," Harmony explained. "Never took a drop of hooch, though he served it."

The man with the rifle stepped up behind Harmony, nudged her with his boot toe. As she glared up at him, he spit chaw in the dust near her thigh. "How come it took you two ladies so long to come after it?"

"None of your goddamn business!" Harmony snapped.

"Don't sass me, girl!" railed the man with the rifle, drawing his hand back threateningly.

Charity grabbed her sister's arm and pulled her back. Her voice was thin, almost confessional. "He didn't tell us about it . . . till he lay dying from his wounds. He didn't want to leave my sister and me destitute."

Standing in the hole, crabbing his right hand toward the walnut grips of his Colt, Fargo remained silent, regarding the Reverend and his cohorts from under the shading brim of his dusty hat.

Charity squinted at the iron-eyed man kneeling beside the hole. "How'd you come to follow us?"

"I was up at the Sunflower camp with my gang of desperadoes here, plannin' a stagecoach job, when I heard the rumor that a saloon owner, who's real name was Three-Gun Pete LeFleur, had swallowed a pill he couldn't digest. I rode into town just as you girls were gettin' ready to ride off with ol' Three-Gun's carcass. Something told me I should follow along, see where you were gonna plant the son of a bitch. Had an inklin' I might just find me a pleasant surprise at the end of the trail."

"Boy, have we!" exclaimed the man to Fargo's left, grinning down at the girls.

Fargo stared up at the man wanly. He'd planted his index and thumb around his pistol's grips. As he began sliding the gun from its holster, the man kneeling before him swung toward him and planted the barrel of his navy Colt against the Trailsman's forehead.

"Go ahead and keep haulin' that iron up out of that holster," the Reverend raked through gritted teeth. "Do it with two fingers. Slow."

Fargo stared at the man's unsettling gray-blue eyes, then did as he was told, handing the pistol over butt-first.

Stuffing the .44 behind his cartridge belt, the Reverend straightened and stepped back from the grave, keeping his own pistol leveled on the Trailsman. "Out."

Fargo glanced at the girls, their faces blanched with fear, and hoisted himself out of the hole.

The Reverend glanced at the four men lined out to his right. "Billy, Price—take 'em off behind the hill, so the shots don't carry to the town."

"No!" Charity lunged toward the leader, her face pinched with fury as she clawed at his face with both hands. She slashed a nail across his lip, drawing blood.

"Bitch!" He grunted, backhanding her. She flew backward into her sister. Harmony caught her halfway to the ground, and they both fell together.

Fargo stared down at Charity, shocked. He hadn't known the brunette had that kind of pluck.

Both girls sobbed in a pile beside the mound of fresh dirt. As the man with the rifle jerked Harmony to her feet, Fargo glanced around. Too many guns were aimed at him to make a move.

"Why kill the girls?" he asked the Reverend. "They're no danger to you."

"They're liable to spill the beans to the army about the missing gold, have troops sent after us." He bunched his lips and shook his head, his eyes glinting with raw evil. "I don't intend to be lookin' over my shoulder the rest of my time here on the good earth. I intend to enjoy myself, spendin' all that money I done bought and paid for with my own sweat and blood."

He glanced at the man with the rifle, who'd gotten both girls to their feet. "Get rid of 'em! Archer, fetch the horses, and we'll start loadin' up this gold."

Archer turned and ran up the hill. "You got it, Reverend!"

Fargo gave the girls another glance, pondering the predicament. Four guns against one unarmed man. How could he finagle a way out of this one?

The man with the Spencer stepped back, rammed a shell into the chamber with a savage grimace, ejecting a spent casing, and aimed the rifle at the Trailsman's chest. "Around behind the hill. You and the girls. Move!"

The man beside him grinned and sidestepped away from him, extending his cocked Remington as he pulled around behind Fargo. He poked his pistol into the Trailsman's back, pushing him forward.

Fargo took two steps toward the girls, stopped, held their gazes, and canted his head at the hill. The girls, wide-eyed and breathing hard, turned reluctantly and began walking, holding their skirts above their ankles.

"Sure are a coupla pretty girls you got there, mister," said the man with the rifle as they strode along the path to the cemetery's rear, angling around graves, rocks, and shrubs. "Bet you been havin' a real good time on the trail."

Fargo said nothing. He watched the men out the corners of his eyes. Both walked about six feet behind him and six feet apart—too far away for him to get a jump on either one.

"Yes, sir!" whooped the man with the pistol. "I sure did envy you back there. I had to share a camp with these three smelly sons o' bitches when you had two buxom fillies at your beck and call." He laughed loudly. "More than once I considered stealin' into your bivouac and gettin' me some!"

"The Reverend wouldn't have none of that." The man with the Spencer kicked a stone and gave a clipped grunt. "The Reverend's a man of *discipline*. Didn't wanna blow our chances of y'all leadin' us to the gold."

"And he was right," the other man allowed.

"Ain't he always?"

Fargo glanced behind. The two were still following about six feet away, six feet apart.

"You oughta let the women go," Fargo said. "Why not keep them for your own pleasure? You said it yourselves—they're a couple of nice pieces of ass. You can always kill 'em later—once you've had your fill."

Both girls jerked flabbergasted looks at Fargo. He said nothing, just continued walking.

His time might be up, but why not try to buy time for the girls? They might have to share the outlaws' bedrolls a time or two, but there was always a chance they'd find a way to escape.

"Nice try, amigo," said the man with the rifle. "A couple tarts like these'd be fun, like you say, but they'd only slow us up."

"You oughta know that!" The other man laughed.

Fargo chuckled dryly, cutting it short when he saw both Harmony and Charity staring at him darkly. He took two more strides. A thought occurred to him.

As he and the girls moved toward the crest of the sun-battered hill, through a stand of spindly piñons and wild mahogany, he stuck two fingers into his mouth, turned his head to one side, and blew.

The whistle echoed loudly.

The man with the Remington rammed its barrel against Fargo's back, a sharp, needling jab that threw the Trailsman forward. "Hey, what the hell you think you're doin'?"

Fargo continued walking, pricking his ears to listen but keeping his eyes straight ahead.

"Hey!" someone shouted behind him.

A half second later, a horse whinnied. Hooves pounded, growing louder. There was the leathery slap of stirrup fenders batting a horse's ribs.

Fargo glanced over his right shoulder.

Beside the grave, the Reverend was staring back toward the front of the cemetery, at the Ovaro stallion galloping toward him, tracing a zigzagging course through some graves and hurdling others. The Reverend slid his pistol from his holster, but before he could raise it, the horse was on him.

The man cursed and dove out of the way as the horse leaped the grave crosswise, hit the ground beyond the dirt mound, shook its head, whinnied, and continued galloping straight toward Fargo's group.

His heart racing anxiously, the Trailsman wheeled

to his right, ignoring the pain in his sore ankle, yelling, "Get down!"

He threw himself into the girls. They went down with a scream. Fargo's shoulder and right hip hit the ground between them. He looked up in time to see the pinto bear down on the desperadoes, who'd turned to see what all the commotion was about.

"Jesus Christ, he's headin' right for us!" yelled the man with the rifle.

He flung himself right while the hardcase with the Remington dove left. The Ovaro put its head down and whinnied, ramming both men as they tried to scramble out of the way, the horse's head and shoulders clipping the men's boots, shoulders, and arms, spinning them both like pinwheels.

As the men windmilled and hit the dirt in dusty, ragged piles, yelling, their hats and weapons flying, the Ovaro ran several yards beyond the group, then turned sideways and stopped. Breathing heavily, the stallion looked at Fargo as if awaiting orders.

Favoring his sprained ankle and glancing at the fallen hardcases, each groaning under separate dust clouds, Fargo heaved himself to his feet.

"Get up!" he yelled at the girls, jerking Harmony to her feet. He grabbed Charity and half dragged both girls toward the pinto. "Get on the horse and haul ass out of here!"

Dusty and bruised, the girls said nothing, but strode purposefully to the horse's left stirrup, knowing this was their only chance of leaving the boneyard alive. Harmony grabbed the horn and leaped into the saddle before reaching down for Charity's outstretched hand.

Fargo shucked his rifle from the saddle boot.

When both girls were on the horse, Harmony stared down at him. "Skye, what about you?"

The Trailsman slapped the pinto's right hip. "Hyaaaah!"

The horse leaped off its rear hooves with a whinny.

Charity gave a shocked grunt and wrapped her arms around Harmony's waist. Then the horse and the girls galloped off to Fargo's right, heading down the hill toward safety.

Peering through their yellow, sifting dust, Fargo squinted his eyes and rammed a shell into the Henry's breech. Ten feet away, both hardcases were climbing heavily to their knees, grunting, their faces bunched with pain. Between them, back down the cemetery hill, the Reverend was running toward them and Fargo, his pistol in his fist.

"Don't let them get away, you goddamn tinhorns!"

18

Braced by the command, both outlaws grabbed their weapons. As they began straightening and swinging toward Fargo, the Trailsman snugged the butt of his Henry against his hip and fired four shots in quick succession, adding powder smoke to the dust fogging the air before him.

Both men stumbled back, screaming, weapons flying, kicking up more dust as they hit the ground at the same time.

Gritting his teeth, Fargo worked the Henry's cocking lever, the smoking brass casing arcing over his right shoulder. He snapped the rifle to his shoulder and stared down the barrel at the Reverend running toward him in a crouch, boots kicking up dust as he zigzagged around rock-mounded graves and crosses. He'd lost his hat, and his string tie flew back behind him.

His mustachioed upper lip stretched back from his teeth. *"Bastard!"*

Fargo fired as the man turned sharply left. The slug knocked a grave marker askance. The Reverend dropped behind another marker and fired.

Fargo threw himself left and rolled off his shoulder.

The Reverend's slug plowed into the gravel behind him.

Rising onto his elbows and aiming the Henry, Fargo sighted down the barrel at the brocade vest sidled up to the wooden cross, and squeezed the trigger.

"Ahhh!" the Reverend screamed on the heels of the rifle's crack.

He fell back behind the cross.

As Fargo rammed another shell into the rifle's chamber, a shadow moved to his right. He rolled left and extended the Henry toward the fourth black-clad gent, who was aiming a rifle at Fargo from atop a boulder at the hill's brushy crown.

The rifle barked, stabbing flames. The slug ricocheted off a rock near Fargo's belly and burned across his cheek. Fargo fired once, levered another quick round, fired again.

Dropping his rifle and clutching his bloody belly, the bushwacker bowed his head, his hat falling as he doubled over and did a somersault off the boulder. He hit the ground with a *whuff*! and a groan, shaking. He landed on his hat and the barrel of his rifle.

Levering the Henry, Fargo jerked a look down the cemetery hill. The Reverend was stumbling back down the grave, heavy footed. Fargo gained his own feet with a grunt and strode down the hill, holding the Henry straight out from his belt.

Near the grave Fargo had dug for Three-Gun Pete, the Reverend stopped and turned back toward the Trailsman. He raised his gun as if it weighed fifty pounds. He fired one round into the ground ten feet before his own boots. The second round plunked into a rock-mounded grave to Fargo's left.

Fargo calmly squeezed the Henry's trigger, watching the man jerk slightly, as if slapped, but remain standing. Fargo levered a fresh round and kept walking, only slightly favoring his sprained ankle.

His lips were set in a hard line, and his lake blue eyes narrowed to slits.

He didn't like being ambushed. Never had. Never would.

"I deserve this money!" shouted the Reverend, his pistol hanging low at his side. He stood, shifting his weight from foot to foot, as if supported by an unseen hand behind him. "You know how long I searched for it?"

Fargo strode toward him, holding the Henry straight out from his right hip.

"I deserve this money! Ol' Three-Gun ran us into a trap and then lit a shuck with the loot! Goddamn it, I *deserve* it!"

He lifted his revolver, stretching his lips back from his bloody teeth as he thumbed back the hammer.

Fargo's Henry barked twice, stabbing flames, the cracks chasing their own echoes around the boneyard.

The Reverend did a bizarre pirouette, head thrown back on his shoulders, arms windmilling, screaming as he dropped into the grave.

Fargo lowered the Henry and hunkered down on his haunches beside the grave. At the bottom, his head lying beside the money sacks, the Reverend lay in a bloody heap. His open, glassy eyes stared up at Fargo dolefully.

Hooves thundered.

Tack squawked.

Fargo turned toward the hill's brow. The girls galloped over it atop the stallion, staring toward him anxiously.

"Skye!" Harmony cried as she drew back on the reins and slid straight down from the saddle. She threw herself into Fargo's arms, pressing her face to his chest. "You're alive!"

In seconds, Charity had dismounted as well, and threw an arm around the Trailsman's waist, staring up at him worriedly. She brushed a thumb along the bullet burn crossing his cheek. "You're injured."

Fargo grinned down at her, pleasantly surprised by the brunette's uncharacteristic ministrations. Her torn blouse had come open again, exposing nearly all of her beguiling but dusty breasts. She'd pressed them to his side, and they made a delicious sight, bubbling up against his belly. A sweat bead was runneling the dirt on her chest, slipping into that dark, deep, forbidden cavern of her cleavage.

Catching his leer, Charity frowned, stepped back, and drew the blouse across her chest. "Savage."

The girls were none too happy when Fargo insisted, once they'd given their father a near-proper burial, that they turn the money over to the local sheriff. The only thing that kept them both from scratching out his eyes was the thousand-dollar reward it turned out the army was offering for the stolen payroll coins.

The greenbacks would get both girls back east, where they'd arranged to be taken in by distant relatives and thus saved from the wretched fate of so many girls who'd found themselves penniless and homeless on the frontier.

The money also put them both up in style in Del Norte's Venus Hotel and Saloon, while they awaited the next stage. It was a five-day wait, and Fargo waited along with them to keep them out of trouble. Of course, it helped that Harmony entertained him as she had along the trail—every chance she could slip away from her pious, watchful sister.

They met so often, in fact, that he was nearly too tired to play poker, his favorite pastime when not on the scouting trail.

Late in the afternoon of their fourth day in Del Norte, Fargo was napping in his own room at the Venus, preparing for a night of five-card-stud, when he heard a key waggle around in his door lock. He lifted his head sharply, reaching for the Colt in the holster hanging from his bedpost.

The smell of cherry-and-lilac perfume wafted from the other side of the door, mingling with the faint smell of burning piñon from the town's braziers and cookstoves. In the last few days, Indian summer had given way to fall.

The Trailsman smiled. He dropped his hand, returned his face to the pillow, and closed his eyes.

He'd given Harmony a key to his room. The tireless blonde was no doubt calling on him one last time before heading to Maryland and, probably, chastity.

What the hell? He could sleep when he was dead.

He near-dozed under the quilt in his big, canopied bed, the window shutters muffling the clomp of hooves and squawk of wagon wheels on the street below.

There was a click as the lock turned. Hinges squawked. The perfume grew stronger, breezing in on the musty air from the hall.

Another click as the door closed.

Fargo drew a deep draft of cherry and lilac, keeping his face in the pillow, listening to the sibilant sounds of a woman undressing, the soft padding of bare feet on the wooden floor and scatter rugs.

Finally, the sheet and quilt were drawn back. A faint chill as the autumn air touched the Trailsman's naked body.

The girl sucked in a sharp breath, as if enervated. She held the sheet and quilt away from him. He felt her eyes on him, touching his body, arousing him. The springs squeaked again, and she crawled in beside him, sliding her body close to his, radiating warmth.

A light hand touched his shoulder.

"Not very careful . . . for the Trailsman." It wasn't Harmony's voice.

Fargo's heart did a somersault.

He jerked his head up, snapping his eyes wide. Before him, reclining on one elbow, her rich auburn hair billowing down over one ear and shoulder, lay Charity.

She hadn't covered herself with the quilts. She lay naked, long legs and rounded ivory hip burnished by the salmon light slipping through the shutters' cracks.

The Trailsman squinted at her, not sure he wasn't dreaming.

"What the hell—?"

She pressed a finger to his lips.

"It kills me to say this, but you're too much man to let get away before . . ." Her voice trailed off. She smiled faintly and lifted a shoulder. "Let's just say it's my way of paying you back for not pestering my sister."

The Trailsman's face warmed. He hoped she couldn't see his flush in the room's murky light.

He cleared his throat. "A gentleman wouldn't take advantage of a young lady's . . . innocence."

"Take advantage of me, Skye! I've been saving myself for marriage . . . but"—her eyes dropped to his shaft, the bulbous head jutting toward her belly button—"that was before I met you. I'm ashamed, but I can't help myself!"

"Nothin' to be ashamed about." Fargo moved toward her, lowered his head to her breasts, fondled the right one in his big brown paw, and suckled the other gently, running his tongue across the nipple. "Only natural."

The nipple stiffened almost instantly, and Charity drew a sharp breath.

She placed her hand on the back of his head, digging her fingers into his hair as she threw her shoulders back, breasts out. Her thin voice quavered. "You won't . . . mutter a word to Harmony?"

Fargo removed his lips from the nipple. "A gentleman doesn't kiss and tell." He resumed chuckling, then suddenly fell silent. "Uh . . . where is your sis, anyway? Wouldn't want her to knock on my door . . . uh . . . lookin' for you."

"Sound asleep," Charity said, pulling his head back to her breasts, fisting his hair in her hands. "She's been unusually tired since arriving in Del Norte. The trip seems to have taken a lot out of her."

"Reckon," Fargo drawled around the nipple in his mouth.

When he had both nipples standing up like small rubber knobs, he lifted his head and gently pushed the girl back toward the pillow.

"Wait." Charity looked up at him, a devilish glint in her wide brown eyes. "Can I be on top? I saw one of the girls doing it that way in Papa's saloon."

Fargo rolled onto his back and crossed his hands behind his head, letting his shaft jut straight up in the air. "That'd work."

She laughed eagerly and climbed onto her hands and knees, catlike, then ran two fingers of her right hand along his iron-hard member from tip to base, smiling down at it like a little girl with a new, forbidden toy.

As she stroked him, making his blood boil, Fargo ran his left hand down her curving back to her firm, rounded butt, the skin smooth as parchment.

Gooseflesh rose, and she shuddered. When he stroked the nap between her legs, she jerked as if chilled, thrusting her chin up and groaning.

Charity removed her fingers from his shaft, glanced at him, bright-eyed, smiling cunningly, then turned back to the engorged rod and closed her lips over it. Her cheeks bulged as she sucked the tip.

Suddenly, she lifted her head, spittle stringing from her lips to the crown of his rod, and crawled on top of him. Wrapping both hands around the shaft, she rose up on her knees.

"Like this?" she whispered.

His voice was pinched with passion. "That should . . . Yeah . . ."

She closed herself over the rod and sank down slowly, letting the shaft inch up into the slick, wet warmth of her. The Trailsman groaned and dug his elbows into the bed, arching his back, closing his hands on her thighs.

It may have been her first time, but the girl had talent. Must run in the family . . .

Charity groaned and shuddered, leaned forward, and kneaded his shoulders. Her hair swept his chest, arousing him even more thoroughly. She tipped her head back and closed her eyes as she rose up and down on his shaft—slowly at first. He rubbed her breasts and lifted his head to lick her nipples.

She moved more quickly, riding him harder and harder. . . .

"Oh, Skye! Oh, Skye!"

He squeezed her round breasts and closed his eyes. "Shh."

"Oh, God!"

"Keep it down. Don't wanna—"

"It feels so *good*!"

Up and down, her body rising and falling, her hair jostling, breasts bobbing. The bed squawked and sang.

"Oh . . . oh . . . oh, Sk—" He closed his hand over her mouth, holding it there as she came, her entire body convulsing, spasming, her screams muffled by his cupped palm.

Gritting his teeth and digging the thumb of his free hand into her thigh, he came with her.

He thought his heart would explode before he'd finished.

It turned out he finished first, then held her until her body gradually stopped quivering and shuddering.

She dropped her head, her thick hair once again sweeping his chest, and lowered her flushed face to his, closing her mouth over his. . . .

They kissed for a long time and cuddled silently until they both grew aroused once more.

157

Before the sun faded from the shutters' cracks, they'd made love nearly every way Fargo knew how to. Charity didn't want to leave, however. She stuck to him like tar until, worried that Harmony would come looking for either one of them and find them both, he helped her dress, then gently shoved her into the hall and closed the door behind her.

He turned away from the door.

A knock.

"Ah, Christ."

He cracked the door. Charity's brown eyes bored into his, glistening with tears. "Skye, what if you've ruined me for every man in the future?"

"Go away." Fargo groaned and yawned. "You're killing me."

He closed the door and stumbled to the bed. A thought occurred to him. He grabbed a chair and wedged it beneath the doorknob.

"Damn fillies're gonna be the death of me yet!"

He flopped onto the bed and fell instantly into a deep, dreamless sleep.

Bright and early the next morning, the girls boarded the stage headed east from Del Norte.

But not before each had kissed the Trailsman good-bye and privately thanked him for not indulging the fleshly curiosities of the other. They waved their gloved hands out the windows as the stage bounded off across the broad San Luis Valley and disappeared over the brow of a low, sage-tufted hill.

Fargo chuckled, yawned, and spurred the Ovaro toward New Mexico.

LOOKING FORWARD!

**The following is the opening
section of the next novel in the exciting
Trailsman series from Signet:**

THE TRAILSMAN #299
DAKOTA DANGER

*Dakota Territory, 1862—nothing is more
dangerous than a man who has lost his
memory—dangerous to himself . . . and to the
killers all around him.*

Traveling through Dakota Territory yesterday, Fargo
had seen two bandits robbing a stage while a third
bandit was busy ripping the clothes off a fetching red-
haired young woman who was obviously a terrified
passenger.

Fargo was on a hill above the stagecoach road.
Squinting against the blistering sunlight, he could see
that the stagecoach driver was sprawled on the

ground, probably dead. That would account for the two shots that had caught Fargo's attention.

Another man, probably riding shotgun, stood with his hands up while one of the bandits shot the lock off a strongbox. The lock took three bullets to smash open.

By this point, the woman had been stripped down to her waist, her sumptuous breasts naked in the daylight as she clawed the punk's face and tried to push him off her.

Fargo used his Henry for this particular job. The first target was the rapist's knee. The shot echoed off the twisted line of prehistoric rock that formed a long wall on the far side of the stagecoach.

The rapist cried out, tried to grab his knee but fell over in pain before his fingers could find the wound.

The next shot smashed the shoulder of the bandit whose gun was pointed at the stagecoach man. His shoulder exploded into flying debris of blood, bone, flesh.

Fargo stood up. "You've had the only chance you're going to get," he said, making his way down the small rocky hill. "I want you to put your hands up and then I want the stagecoach man to pick up your guns. You make any kind of move and you're dead."

They dropped their guns in the dirt.

The first thing the stagecoach man did was check on his partner. He knelt down next to the body. But it was clear pretty quickly that his friend was no longer alive.

He raised angry eyes to one of the bandits and then stood up. "He was gonna be fifty years old tomorrow, you son of a bitch."

The rapist obviously hoped that Fargo had been distracted by the bitter words. His hand shot out as he tried to grab the woman again. She had just managed to cover herself with the torn parts of her blouse.

She screamed and lurched away the moment she felt the bandit's hand on her.

Fargo executed the man. He had given clear warning but the man had elected to disregard Fargo's words. The execution came swiftly. The bandit's forehead bloomed with a huge red flower of blood.

Both of the other highwaymen decided that this would be their last chance for freedom. One of them dove for his gun in the road.

He caught a bullet in his temple.

The other man had his gun in his hand by now. He got off two quick shots at Fargo. But he was too scared to fire with any care. The shots went wide. Fargo got him directly in the heart.

Before the echoes of gunfire had quite faded, the stagecoach man walked out from behind the horses and watched as Fargo approached. "Sure glad you showed up, mister. I would've been dead for sure. This is a bad bunch. They've killed two people in the last couple weeks."

The woman came up then.

She was obviously a female of breeding. The white blouse was real silk and the dark blue skirt looked custom-tailored. A thin bracelet on her slender left wrist was gold. "I'm sure glad you came along, too. He would've killed me after he was done with me. Or maybe all of them would've spent some time with me—and then killed me." She smiled. "I'd shake your hand but then the front of my blouse would fall down and you've both seen enough of me, I'm afraid."

Never enough of you, Fargo thought.

"If you'd be so kind," she said to the stagecoach man, "and take the brown leather bag from up top. I've got a couple of blouses in there I could wear."

That had been Fargo's introduction to Amy Fenton. And what an introduction it had been.

Excerpt from DAKOTA DANGER

*   *   *

Amy spent the next morning at the bank she'd inherited from her father. She dragged Fargo along to
see the town of Tall Rock. He was all shaved up and
shiny and she didn't hesitate to show him off as the
trophy he was. She was not only the only female bank
president in the Territory, she didn't bother to hide
the fact that as a young woman she still had plenty of
appetite for good times and pleasure.

Fargo had been traveling for nearly ten days
straight before he met Amy at the robbery scene, so
after she was done showing him off and had set
about her business, Fargo went up to her vice president, a prim little man named David Culver. He was
as stiff as his celluloid collar. His displeasure with
Fargo could be read on his face. His expression was
that of a man who'd found himself standing in pig
feces on a very hot day.

Culver wore a gold cross on his lapel. He wanted
everybody to know that he was morally superior to
them. Fargo figured that the small man probably was.
Just about everybody, at least as Fargo saw it, was
morally superior to Skye Fargo.

"I was wondering if you could direct me to the general store and the gunsmith's shop," Fargo asked
pleasantly.

"They're really not very difficult to find," the man
said. "The whole business district is three blocks long.
They're not all that hard to find."

"Well," Fargo said, "I appreciate the information."

The man leaned forward, spoke in a whisper.
"You're not the first, you know. She parades you saddle tramps in and out of here like a slave auction."

Fargo smiled. "Interesting you won't tell me where
the general store is but you'll tell me about your boss's
personal life."

"I'm giving you a warning is all. I just hate to think you'd fall in love or something. I'm just talking man-to-man."

The "man-to-man" remark left Culver wide-open to a nasty crack from Fargo. But Fargo was tough, not mean.

Fargo spent an hour on his errands, and by that time Amy was waiting for him at the office of the Badlands Express, another business she'd inherited from her father. A four-vehicle stagecoach company.

The pride and joy of her fleet was a new-model Concord that was presently the most lavish coach constructed for commercial use. She was excited about showing it to Fargo.

This one was painted bright red. The interior was sleek polished wood with leather-covered benches that could seat eight people comfortably. The horses were already in their traces. Amy had changed clothes. The suit she'd worn had been replaced by a chambray shirt, Levi's, and a pair of hand-tooled riding boots. She was somehow even more elegant in these duds than in her more formal ones.

The round-trip she described would take just under two hours, she told Fargo.

Even with all the new types of support mechanisms, a stagecoach ride was still a stagecoach ride, though it was less violent than most of the coaches Fargo had ridden in. At least you didn't get thrown from one side to the other, or crack your head on the ceiling.

Of all the places Fargo had seen on his travels, none compared to the Badlands. Illustrations of prehistoric times were fashionable these days but none could capture the strangeness of the land that rose up on either side of him. Steep cliffs, ragged ravines, rock formations that startled the eye, and colors Fargo had never seen before.

Not hard to imagine that giant flying predators had once dominated this land eons ago.

Or even that dinosaurs had prowled its spiky crests and twisted rock spires.

"Now I'll be the teacher and you be the student, all right, Skye?"

She wasn't the sort of woman to wait for a man's approval.

She plunged right into her lecture about the history of the Badlands, how neither the Indians nor the French had been able to conquer them. To the south of the Badlands was soil so rich, farmers barely needed to plant. Whites and Indians alike prospered there.

But here . . .

Finished with her history lecture, Amy leaned out the coach window and said, "Give the horses a workout, Riley!"

"Yes'm," the driver called down to her. "You just hold on to your bonnet."

She pulled her head back in. "Someday I'm going to wear a bonnet and surprise old Riley." She gave Fargo an impish smile. "In fact, maybe I'll wear a bonnet to bed tonight. I hope you'll be there to see it."

"Fine by me," Fargo said. "As long as that's all you wear."

But there was no more time for flirtatious conversation because suddenly Riley lost control of the stagecoach and it veered sharply to the right and inched off the narrow rock road.

The screams of the horses were terrible to hear.

Even more terrible was the knowledge that coach and passengers alike were about to plunge into fast-churning water in the deep ravine below.

Fargo hit the top of the door with such force that he blacked out instantly.

No other series has this much historical action!

THE TRAILSMAN

S310

GRITTY HISTORICAL ACTION FROM

USA TODAY BESTSELLING AUTHOR

RALPH
COTTON

Available wherever books are sold or at
penguin.com

S909

Signet Historical Fiction

Ralph Cotton

The Big Iron Series

Jurisdiction

0-451-20547-2

Young Arizona Ranger Sam Burrack has vowed to bring
down a posse of murderous outlaws—and save the
impressionable young boy they've befriended.

**Available wherever books are sold or at
penguin.com**